Karlovy Vary Goodbye

Karlovy Vary Goodbye

ŠTĚPÁN NOVÁK

The Book Guild Ltd

First published in Great Britain in 2022 by
The Book Guild Ltd
9 Priory Business Park
Wistow Road, Kibworth
Leicestershire, LE8 0RX
Freephone: 0800 999 2982
www.bookguild.co.uk
Email: info@bookguild.co.uk
Twitter: @bookguild

Typeset in 11pt Adobe Garamond Pro

Printed and bound in Great Britain by 4edge Limited

ISBN 978 1914471 025

British Library Cataloguing in Publication Data.
A catalogue record for this book is available from the British Library.

For my parents

Preface

This novel is a combination of memory and fiction. The events described in Parts One and Two belong to twentieth- and twenty-first-century history.

All locations are factual. The names of well-known public figures in the story have been retained. All other identities have been changed.

"Of my nation? What is my nation?"

HENRY V. ACT 3. SCENE 2. MACMORRIS.
WILLIAM SHAKESPEARE. 1599.

*"Everyman is a piece of the continent.
A part of the main."*

DEVOTIONS UPON EMERGENT OCCASIONS.
JOHN DONNE. 1624.

"In my beginning is my end."

FOUR QUARTETS. 'EAST COKER'.
T.S. ELIOT. 1943.

PART ONE

1938–1960

1

Spring 1938

THE WHITE ROOM was so high that a swing had been hung from the ceiling, halfway between his bed and the veranda doors. He tried to open his eyes. The swing's ropes were dark, vertical lines against the morning light. He closed his eyes again and all became an even blue.

Still waking, he curled his toes. At last, fully conscious, he threw aside the bedclothes and leapt to the veranda. The rooftops of the town below were covered by an early mist, which rose slowly past the villa and up into the pine trees. He ran to the top of the staircase and shouted down all three storeys: "Žophie, Žophie, how soon are we going out?"

Although he spoke to his parents in a combination of Czech and German, with Žophie he used only Czech. He could hear her short breaths as she slowly climbed the stairs. Žophie was not young. Her wrinkled face appeared over the banisters.

"Jan, Jan, go and wash, put on your clothes and come down to breakfast."

He ran along the corridor to the bathroom, made a pretence of washing his face and hands, then back to his room. He jumped around as he put on the clothes which Žophie had laid out.

On the first floor his parents were already having breakfast. They would leave early for the surgery where they both worked. His mother hugged him; his father made a joke, then continued to talk to his mother about Schopenhauer. At breakfast especially, but at other meals too, his father tended to talk about Schopenhauer or Nietzsche or Kant or Hegel, though he himself was a dentist. Everyone found that such conversation suited him.

Even as the boy was relishing bread, ham, cheese and milk, his parents stood up to leave. His mother hugged him again. His father joked again. Then both were gone. The surgery work would last all day; there were many important visitors in the spa town, visitors from America, England, Germany and Russia. All would be taking the waters, the mud baths, the colonic irrigation sessions. Many also wanted to have dental treatments.

Hearing Žophie's steps on the landing, Jan ran across the room and threw himself into her apron. He loved his Žophie, perhaps even more than he loved his mother and father. His questions flew at her: "Can we go out? When can we go? Where shall we go? Can we go up into the forest?"

Žophie tut-tutted. She had a warm smile. She was carrying an overcoat and a scarf and held her walking stick. At first, the woods would be damp and slippery. She gave Jan a small rucksack with a pullover, a bottle with water and a chocolate bar.

They left the villa and began to climb. Within fifty metres they reached the woodland, which continued to rise steeply further up the hillside. Žophie walked carefully.

The boy knew the woods well, running forwards and backwards, taking side loops along unused tracks, through open glades, jumping over roots, fallen branches and old tree stumps. He rested only to pluck and eat the new crop of wild strawberries. Sometimes he shouted to Žophie about a discovery he had made, maybe a deep burrow or a dead rabbit. It was at a moment when Žophie's steady pace placed her ahead of himself on their route, that he saw the woman. She was sitting about five metres above the ground, balancing on the horizontal branch of a pine tree. She wore black. He knew at once that she was a witch. He also knew that he was awake. He stumbled past her, stopped, then looked back. The woman was silent, her face contorted as she stared at him, her mouth open, with her tongue hanging forward, childlike, her fist shaking at him again and again. What had he done? He continued to stand still, looking at her. Then, very fast, he stuck out his tongue in her direction. He turned rapidly and ran on.

Over the remainder of the walk, he was quieter. He said nothing to Žophie. For the rest of his life, he would remember the woman in the tree. Was she real or was she just a part of his imagination? What did her presence mean?

The family meal that evening began quietly. His mother and father, partners at work in the dental surgery, had returned home together and had made caring small talk with him, enquiring about his day. His account missed out the story of the woman in the tree; it was so unbelievable. Cook had prepared his favourite: Wiener schnitzel with sauté potatoes and spinach. At mealtimes his father was usually lively, filling their conversations with affectionate quips directed towards his wife and young son, who would both respond with equal pleasure. That evening, however, Ivan ate in comparative silence, glancing from time to time at his watch and towards a radio on the dining-room sideboard. At a particular moment near the end of the meal, he rose to switch on a programme.

At once, the quiet room was filled with a crackling and roaring and thundering, alien to the boy's comprehension. The totality of the sounds came in waves, which he now made out to be thousands of voices in unison, each wave responding to a single man's voice, the latter beginning slowly, staccato, harsh, accusing, grating, bitter, then gathering momentum to become a screech, a challenge, an order, as the roar of the listeners began to respond, a roar in turn swelling to a crescendo, then obediently dying away as the lone voice took over again. The duet between orator and audience continued to fill the dining room until his father, who had remained standing, switched off the radio and sat down again.

All three now sat in silence. The boy asked what was happening. His mother looked towards his father, who tried to smile.

"Across the border, Chancellor Hitler thinks that our country belongs to Germany. Well, it does not."

Jan waited for his father to say more but no further amplification came.

Instead, his mother said, "Don't worry," though he hadn't been worrying, and she continued, "Tomorrow is my free workday. We will go out and enjoy ourselves. Go to bed now, dear."

The discussion was over before it had really begun. As he went upstairs, the boy could still hear his parents continuing to talk quickly. His father's voice became clear at intervals: "Four hundred thousand troops even now at the border... our Beneš has no choice... partial mobilisation now... so far the younger ones... probably more soon..."

Jan always looked forward to Thursdays. Every Thursday, his mother did not go to work. Instead, his father would leave alone for the surgery, Žophie would have a free day, and Ilona and her son would together enjoy the life of the town.

That summer morning of 1938 was no different from the other summer Thursdays he could remember. The day's typical routine had a calm certainty, which the five-and-a-half-year-old enjoyed. They started early, with Jan skipping down the front steps and running ahead along Imperial Street towards the funicular railway stop, which lay parallel to the villa on the hillside contours. The boy flung himself into one of the worn wooden seats of the single carriage and waited impatiently for the sound of the operating bell, a signal from the town stop below. Then, with many jolts, the carriage dropped on its rack-and-pinion track through a dark hillside tunnel down to the valley floor. He knew that his parents' working days also always began with the same three-minute journey.

The carriage had hardly come to a halt, with the door safety latches just opened, when he again ran ahead of his mother down a winding, electrically lit tunnel and out into the morning haze.

Before them, the Baroque and Art Nouveau buildings of the old town stretched left and right along each bank of the river Tepla, its waters flowing between stone retaining walls. To the left, just as the Tepla curved out of sight, a group of flags hung limply outside the long frontages of the Grandhotel Pupp, still covered in shadow from background hillsides and pinewoods. To the right stretched the long vista of the *kurpromenade*, ending in the distance at the white church of St Mary Magdalene. The valley had not yet sprung to life. Under the trees, alongside hotel forecourts, horse-drawn carriages waited, their drivers idle, the horses' nostrils snorting steamy webs into the cool morning air. The town's visitors were evidently still experiencing the flavours of hotel breakfast or the rigours of sanatorium fasting. Only a few eager cure-seekers were already active, filling their beakers with the famous thermal springwater which gushed endlessly upwards from its underground source through the spouting fountains which lined the promenade.

At this stage of the morning, the pair walked together, or rather his mother walked, disappearing at intervals into local shops to buy provisions for a picnic or to browse momentarily in expensive china stores, while the boy ran and climbed and then ran again, shouting for echoes from roof overhangs as they moved northward through the Thermal Spring, Chateau and Market Colonnades. Within the stonework of the largest, the Mill Colonnade, an orchestra group was already starting to set up for the daily Viennese concert which would entertain lunchtime crowds. For the moment, the musicians had time to tease the boy, to exchange greetings with the attractive mother.

His mother had told him how, in the last years of the old Austro-Hungarian empire before the Great War, she had played as a girl with her friends on the terraced roof of the Mill Colonnade. Now she and those very same friends, now also mothers, met with their children for Thursday morning coffee outings at the same café on the same terrace in their same hometown.

Two of his mother's friends, Lenka and Eva, were already there, enjoying coffee and cakes. Their children (Lenka had two boys – six-year-old twins Tomas and Libor – while Eva had a five-year-old daughter Johana) were playing tag at the south end of the terrace, where Jan immediately ran over to join them. The children's antics provoked minimal glances from the three women, who were soon deep in conversation, a part continuation of their last meeting. The sequence of these discussions was often similar each week. At first, the immediate activities of all three families were covered: what they had done last weekend and during those last few days, who had played evening tennis at the Hotel Imperial courts and with whom, who had been to the horse racing, whose husbands had taken time off for golf and, as for this coming weekend, who would be at the theatre on Saturday night and would anybody be willing to meet at the park concert on Sunday afternoon or, alternatively, what about some swimming at the thermal open-air pool?

There followed, as usual, the latest appraisal of the state of the town: how this year's season was again bringing in the international set, the English nobility, the old Russian émigrés, the new American spenders. Jan's mother confirmed that surgery appointments were fully booked until September, that clients were again combining specialist dental treatments with other spa treatments. But after the summer, she asked, what then? What was happening to Europe? For once, the three women paused. Along the terrace, the children's laughter continued.

Eva was complacent. "Why should anything change? After all, the hot springs will continue to go on gushing two hundred litres of hot water out of the ground every minute of every day. Miracle waters for bathing, curative waters for drinking." She became even more dramatic. "For six hundred years, ever since Charles IV's hunting party, the elite of Europe have visited our town. Royalty, aristocracy and the famous have kept on returning: Frederick the Great, Maria Theresa, Franz Joseph, Metternich, Bismarck, Goethe, Schiller, Mozart, Beethoven, Brahms, Liszt, Schumann, Weber, Wagner, Richard Strauss, and more latterly, Freud and Gustav Klimt…" She was almost breathless. "The list continues! The Hotel Pupp is still one of the world's Grand Hotels. The town is so pretty, the woodlands and walks so magnificent. Why should all of this stop? Why be so pessimistic?"

Lenka disagreed. "You can be optimistic, Eva. You are safe. Your parents are part of that Bohemian German generation that gives Chancellor Hitler his excuse to invade. He says there are three and a half million people like you who need to be rescued. You mention only the German and Austrian visitors. That's probably why you miss out other world leaders, particularly from my side, the east, the Czars like Peter the Great and his wife Catherine, the writers like Turgenev, Gogol and Tolstoy, the composers like Tchaikovsky and Chopin and, of course, our very own Dvořák, who premiered his New World Symphony in this place. It's all so different for my family. You know that my grandfather was a Czech factory worker. He would never have been able, nor would he have wanted, to fraternise with your grandfather. Now you and I and our children are all friends, equals, but Herr Hitler, if he comes, might have different ideas."

Ilona tried to bring her friends together. "I come from both sides. You know that my mother's mother, who came from a Hungarian farming family, married an Austrian army cavalry officer. Together, they were true representatives of that great Austro-Hungarian empire which finally disappeared twenty years ago. Now we have our new country, fashioned out of the old melting pot. Surely, we should all stay close together, work together, supporting each other's lives in our beautiful town? Surely, we don't want, don't need, Herr Hitler to tell us how to live."

Lenka could not be eased out of her growing depression. "Maybe we do need a big shake-up! You know, I've never been able to go along with what this place really stands for, this subservience to aristocracy, to the famous and the rich. We fawn over them. We also cheat them, which I don't like either, as we pretend to cure their diabetes, their gout, their ailing livers and gallbladders. We even tell them that the thermal springs are a cure against premature ageing. What rubbish! They should be less dissolute, then they might live longer. At least Ilona here actually repairs their rotting teeth. As for the spa water, can't you see how it's corroding even the spouts on the fountains? So, what is it doing to people's insides? I've never understood how anyone could drink the revolting stuff. Perhaps one day we will be more truthful to our guests. Perhaps one day we will also cater more for ordinary working people and so be truthful to ourselves."

At this point, Jan and his three friends had run back, announcing that they were still hungry. Two other mothers with children had also suddenly arrived. The discussions faded, perhaps to be continued on the following Thursday.

Ilona said that she and Jan were going to have a picnic. Her son eagerly offered to carry the provisions. He ran ahead of his mother all the way southwards, back along the riverbank to a second funicular, which lay behind the Hotel Pupp. This second rack-and-pinion track pulled their carriage straight up into the trees. As they rose, the boy's hunger combined with his sense of the surrounding forest silence, the green freshness of the hillside, the smell of pine cones and pine needles, the bursts of sunlight on open glades. Life was good.

They alighted with others at the cable-car station called Diana's Tower. Even here, they did not change their established routine.

"Wait, wait, I won't be long." Jan ran to the door at the foot of the stone lookout tower, a relic of imperial hunting days. Inside the small hallway was the start of a flight of stairs. He jumped onto the bottom stair and began to climb, as he had done every Thursday lunchtime. He could climb the hundred and fifty risers to the top viewing platform in four minutes, scarcely taking in the panorama of surrounding hills before bounding back down to where his mother was patiently waiting. Then, they would walk along wood-lined tracks until they reached an open resting place, preferably with a distant view. Here, they would finally settle to eat, drink and talk. Sometimes he fell asleep in the sunshine while his mother read a book.

The return home from mid-afternoon onwards was equally dependable. There was the descent into the valley, a two-hour diagonal crossing and recrossing of the woodland routes, his chance for further exploration and adventure. Down in the town, there was a choice of bridges across the Tepla to reach the foot of the morning's funicular journey. By this time, queues were forming as townspeople left their places of work to ride upwards and homewards. Jan and his mother would usually reach the villa before his father, a workaholic, arrived for the evening meal.

For the boy, the summer months of 1938 remained permanently sunlit, unhurried and idyllic. The life of the town changed regularly through its seasonal calendar. Everything was prepared for the cures and comforts of the visitors. Timetables were posted on sanatorium and hotel noticeboards, indicating private health treatments held behind closed doors. There were changing programmes of theatre, opera and lunchtime recitals, as well as dates of racecourse meetings, tennis tournaments, art gallery launches, park concerts and countryside festival days. The visitors, many of them elderly and declining in health, moved in slow motion through the streets, squares, shops and public buildings. On café restaurant terraces, one could witness the unheeding destruction of so many carefully programmed personal diets.

Through June, July and August, the life of Jan's family also progressed in an established sequence. Thursdays were still anchor days. On other weekdays, his parents tended to be away together at the surgery for long hours. This was normal; it was the season. Jan would be independently active, going to kindergarten on three mornings a week (only seven-year-olds started real school) and playing with his many friends at their homes or at the villa, where Žophie was always a supporting hand.

Sometimes, days would become extra special when his grandmother, his mother's mother, arrived, usually without earlier warning or announcement. Magda Dunai, the eldest daughter of a Hungarian farming family, had left home in her late teens to study in Prague. There, she became a linguist and columnist for the *Prager Tagblatt*, before marrying the Austrian officer who died soon after their daughter Ilona was born. Now long retired and living in an apartment in the town, Magda would travel by funicular to the hillside station, from where she would walk slowly to the villa, always accompanied by her English greyhound, Pretty. On the arrival of the haughty, elegant woman, always so perfectly attired, the whole household would become immediately attentive, fortunately sighing with relief as Magda, Pretty and Jan moved away on their customary hillside promenade which always formed the centre point of the visit. The unusual perambulating trio became a memorable group in the hillside landscape, a tall, calm, erect figure looking forever outwards to vistas across the valley, while a small, excited figure at her side fussed over the thin, doleful-eyed canine guardian whom the boy evidently adored.

Family weekend activities varied. On occasions, Jan and his father would walk together in the woods, both content within the silent landscape to be silent in each other's company. At weekends, the family of three joined for late breakfasts, which were prepared by his mother because Petra, the cook, was away. These breakfasts were happy occasions, not least because neither of his parents mentioned dentistry, nor did his father bring up the subject of Herr Hitler. Instead, his father's favourite subjects for conversation continued to be the philosophers, all of whom seemed to be attendant at the table. Even though the boy did not properly understand philosophical concepts, he could see that his mother was encouraging his father to throw thoughts and ideas into the air because they were allowing her man to be light-hearted and light-headed, conditions which then quickly spread to them all.

Yet, it was in the evenings of late August that Jan would find his father in a more sombre mood. When the boy looked for his father to say goodnight, he would sometimes find Ivan sitting alone next to the wireless set, listening intently to the sound, turned low.

Then, on an early evening in September, Jan found Ilona and Ivan standing in front of the wireless. This time the sounds were much louder. The boy stood by his parents.

"It's him again, isn't it? All those up-and-down waves, like day and night! First his voice and then a breath and then thousands of voices together and then him all over again!"

"Yes, it's him," Ivan quietly answered. "All that noise is coming from Nuremberg in Germany. The Nazi party are having what they call a rally. They are celebrating the German takeover of Austria. They have us all in their sights."

On the following day, Jan's grandmother made an unexpected evening visit. She made a decisive announcement to the family: "I shall shortly be leaving to spend the winter in the south of France. Our snow and ice suits me less and less. I have booked my usual room in the Monte Carlo boarding house. I will play bridge with my friends through the winter season."

They did not try to hold her back. Only Jan protested when it was decided that Pretty should go into kennels.

September continued to be hot. His grandmother's departure and Pretty's absence seemed to affect his parents, who responded less to his boisterous antics, though his father did still play the game of 'throwing Jan in the air' with him. After the evening meal, Jan would again often find Ivan sitting alone in the dining room listening to the radio which had been turned down, though it was still possible to hear many incoming voices as well as 'that man' in the background. There were other moments when his parents would talk lengthily behind the closed door of their bedroom, his mother asking questions, his father's answering voice deep and calm and measured.

From mid-September onwards, the mornings became cooler. Ilona persuaded Jan to put on warmer clothing for the regular Thursday outing to the Mill Colonnade. The town's health-giving season was ending. There were fewer foreign visitors in the streets. The string orchestra, in its walled location, continued to perform strenuously but only to random passers-by. At the Colonnade coffee-time meeting, Jan and his friends played unhindered on the upper terrace while their parents' attention was being taken up in argument. Meanwhile, in the town park, new groups were congregating to listen to new kinds of visiting speakers who gesticulated wildly, arms flailing, their speeches hoarse with passion, encouraging listeners to interrupt with equal emotional responses.

In the villa, the radio announcements now continued daily, often to an empty dining room. Each day became more fragmented, with outings postponed as Jan's parents concentrated their activities randomly between surgery and home. On the third Friday of the month, Ivan came home early. Jan, embracing his father, heard Ivan tell Ilona, "It is today. You may have heard the bulletin. General Jan Syrový has announced general mobilisation for all classes up to the age of forty years."

"But, my dear, you are forty-five. And besides, you did your fighting as a young man in the Great War."

"Oh, I just slept a lot in the Italian Alps, like a good Czech soldier Švejk." Then he was clear: "Now, let us just get ready."

During the last seven days of September, Ivan was away from home for long periods. "On errands," Ilona said. She herself appeared self-engrossed. Even Žophie had little time for the boy while she fussed over household jobs. Jan and two of his friends romped in the villa garden on mornings and afternoons. Only at the evening meal would his parents ask attentively about his day's activities.

On the morning of Friday 30th September, Jan's father had left early for the surgery. For some reason, Ilona remained at home. She said that she had things to do. Apparently, the kindergarten's morning session had been cancelled. For much of the day, Jan was again left to his own devices, so he went to test out new acrobatic movements on his bedroom swing.

In the late afternoon, his mother called him to come down to the ground floor. His father was standing in the lounge. Ilona had also fetched Petra, Pavlina and Žophie. Jan's face was full of questions. Ivan asked everyone to sit down. His voice was clear.

"Dear everyone, during this afternoon you may have heard the radio news... that our homeland has been signed away. Today in Munich, the representatives of Germany, Italy, France and England have together signed an agreement which has ceded our side of Czechoslovakia, maybe a third of the country, to Germany. Yes, Jan, 'ceded'. 'Given away' would have more meaning. We know that a massed German army has been waiting across the border for weeks. This agreement allows the Germans to take over on 10th October, but I think that invasion can happen any day now. Their secret supporters must already be waiting in our town."

Ivan swallowed hard before continuing.

"Our country had no part in this agreement. The English Prime Minister, Chamberlain, has always described our situation as 'a quarrel in a faraway country between people of whom we know nothing'. Earlier today, that man Chamberlain flew into London waving a piece of paper in the air and boasting 'Peace in our Time' and 'Peace with Honour'. This Prime Minister of a nation which, together with France, had promised to protect us. Instead, they have betrayed us."

Ivan steadied himself again.

"When I reached the surgery this morning, three of the four technicians were already waiting. They must have been German sympathisers all along. Their usual white smocks were now brown uniforms. All gave Nazi salutes with loud *zieg heils*. I was in shock for a moment and just stood there. 'You must return our salutes,' they said. 'I am a Czech,' I said. 'I don't salute like you.' They said, 'Salute or we shoot you.' 'Then shoot me,' I said. Then they started to laugh and became very polite. 'Herr Doktor Dusek,' they said, 'you will come to see that this is a great day. The Führer has plans for us all. You have nothing to fear. You and the Frau Doktor have been good to us, you were always Czechs in harmony with your Sudeten German neighbours, so we will of course support you. Naturally, we regret that you are a member of your Czech National Socialist Party but then so also are many of your friends. And although we are aware that you are not now a religious man, your protestant upbringing will absolve you from further enquiries. So please, Herr Doktor, please join us.' Again, they saluted and spouted their *zieg heil* and their *heil Hitler*." His father paused again.

"We had apparently already been checked. All of us. I told them that I would go home to decide what to do, that I would in all likelihood return on Monday morning for work. Of course, I will not be there. Later today I will leave to enlist in the Czech army; reservists like me are being called up to support our main army which was fully mobilised a week ago. The Russians have promised to send troops through Romania to help us; perhaps together we may be able to push the Germans back."

He turned to Žophie, Petra and Pavlina. "My wife and

Jan will temporarily go to Prague till this is resolved and we will then all three return to you. Žophie, you will have the keys. Petra and Pavlina, please continue with Žophie to look after the villa. Here is money for all of you for many months. I hope it will be enough. Žophie, this is an additional sum for you since you have agreed to take Pretty from the kennels and look after her."

Žophie was trembling. Petra was rolling her eyes. Pavlina was weeping. Ilona remained composed.

It was only much later, when Jan was grown up, that he wondered at the naivety of his father's plans. Had this intelligent doctor, this would-be philosopher, really imagined a scenario involving a return? Perhaps he had not really believed any such thing but had to propel himself and others into action of whatever kind, but action at least rather than inertia.

For much of the rest of the day, the boy hung around, intrigued by the speed of the adults' comings and goings. The wireless was now switched off. Decisions had to be carried out. Last phone calls had to be made. His father went out on one further errand, then returned. Presents were given to the three keepers of the villa. Pavlina continued to weep. Some papers were burnt in the grate. Two small photograph albums were found. Just before it was getting dark, his father embraced his mother, then lifted the boy high into the air.

"See you soon, my son. Look after your mother. Be strong."

Some moments later, a car drove him away.

A short night followed. Jan slept soundly, a habit that would later serve him well at any time and in any place. It was only in the early hours of the next morning, the first day of October, that a dull thumping somewhere in the background of his dreams coaxed him slowly into daylight. The thumps continued, some singly, some in pairs or even in multiple groups. He could see the bedroom swing dangling erratically, as if pushed by an unseen hand. At the next thump, the bedroom chairs shook.

His mother came into the room, carrying some clothes. She kissed him. "Wash your face, dear, get dressed and come down quickly."

On his way downstairs, he noticed open doors and rooms tidier than usual. When he reached the dining room, Žophie and his mother were already drinking coffee together and talking quietly. On the table were croissants, fruit and milk. He started eating. He was waiting for explanations, but none came. In the silences between thumps, all was quiet; it seemed that no one else was in the house. Žophie kept looking towards him, then looking away.

When he had finished a glass of milk, his mother stood up. "Dearest, you and I are going away today. We'll soon be back. Žophie will look after everything."

As Žophie fumbled with the table crockery, his mother guided him into the next room. On the floor was a small suitcase, hardly bigger than a briefcase. On its brown and black leather surfaces were travel labels from his parents' honeymoon, with images and names of distant places: Merano, Milan, Florence, Capri, Taormina... Next to the case was his own small mountain rucksack which he had used for skiing trips since his birth (he had been able to ski before he could walk), as well as his mother's sling handbag and his own and her winter coats.

"We can wear the coats," she said. "It's not too warm." She helped him, unnecessarily, with his coat and rucksack. "We must go now."

Žophie reappeared, hesitating. Then she engulfed him, coat and rucksack and all, with her trembling old body. She had that Žophie smell which he had always known, a mixture of talcum powder and lilac. She was repeating: "Jan, my little Jan, *muj maly chlapec*," over and over. His mother waited. Then, she placed a hand on Žophie's shoulder and, as the boy stepped back, it was his mother's turn to embrace her old friend. Then, his mother also stepped back, repeating, "We must go now."

At the front door she said again, "We will be back as soon as possible." Did either of the women believe it? Then mother and son were out in the street and walking towards the funicular station. Jan looked back several times, waving to the bent figure in the shadow of the doorway. After the next bend in the road, Žophie was gone.

Other people, more than usual, were also moving towards the funicular. All were carrying cases and bundles, some so large and heavy as to make movement slow. He and his mother overtook them. At the hillside station, a large gathering waited for the carriage to come up from the valley. Many people were pointing to the smoke which was drifting into the sky above the pinewoods, beyond the Hotel Pupp.

A woman said, "They broke through at the border west of Cheb; the guns are so close now," as more thumps shook the station railings.

"But are we winning?" asked a second woman.

And another: "Traitors and collaborators are already in charge."

When the empty carriage arrived, there was a scramble. His mother, a slight figure, seemed possessed of a strength he had not noticed before. Her determination ensured them both a place in the back row of the carriage, which started moving down into the tunnel even as more passengers were attempting to jump on.

In the valley, the streets alongside the Tepla were already crowded. On each bank, a stream of people was moving northwards, men, women, children, all age groups, the majority carrying an assortment of belongings, some of which were already being dropped and left as litter in the confusion.

Jan was full of curiosity. "Where are we going?"

"To the railway station. Now, just keep up with me."

They were accustomed to walking together; it was almost like a Thursday, except for the crowds. As Jan pushed ahead, he could see the world from the waist height of surrounding grown-ups, his face pressed against assortments of clothing and baggage. He looked up past heads and shoulders to see the clouds overhead, which were also moving fast, either covering the ground scene with a spread of heavy grey or parting suddenly to throw sunlight and shadow into the streaming people. By now, the earlier gunfire noises began to be accompanied by a succession of crackling sounds, which reminded the boy of firework displays on the last evening of the Karlovy Vary summer festival.

"Machine guns," a man shouted. "They've reached the Hotel Pupp."

To the airborne sounds was added a dense overall humming, the merging of hundreds of voices, asking questions, giving assurances, directing, complaining, with bodies panting for breath, twisting, turning, pushing, pulling, holding, with families attempting to stay close together or losing touch, with the elderly clutching each other or being supported by relatives or strangers. The swell of people carried itself forwards. As they reached the Mill Colonnade, Jan looked across the water to the Vridelni bank. Lights had been switched on in his parents' surgery at Műlbrun Ulice. He turned to tell his mother, but she was already striding ahead, knowing that he would follow.

Soon, they negotiated the bend by Dvořák Park, then north again along the stretch called Svobozeni against Smetana Park, a green and peaceful location where morning rows of horses, carriages and coachmen had waited patiently under the trees for the arrival of day visitors from Prague. No horses or visitors this time, just an avenue of leafless trees edging the escaping townspeople.

Above the trees in the distance ahead, wisps of smoke were beginning to be seen drifting over the roofs of the railway station. This indication of the possible departure of a train prompted more desperation, as members of the crowd tried to run forwards faster, even while carrying heavy loads. More people began to be pushed over, calling or crying, among mixtures of discarded suitcases, packages, even walking sticks, while those behind stepped over or around them. Self-preservation unified all: must get away... at any cost... no matter where... no matter what... now... now...

As Jan held back to take in the scene, his mother turned, gripped his elbow and pulled him towards their last obstacle: the Thalmanuv Bridge, which spanned the River Ohře at its junction with the Tepla. On the long but narrow crossing, all momentum was momentarily blocked, side to side, by a width of straining bodies. Jan did not see how the blockage suddenly cleared, yet within seconds, his mother was on the station approach side, guiding him ahead through the clamour towards a train which seemed to be already overflowing with people.

His mother moved purposefully ahead to pull at a door handle. Jan could see only legs, cases, bags, blankets, pillows. Ilona part-lifted, part-pushed him upwards. Someone's arm from within a compartment pulled him in. He could feel his mother's knees against his back, a man's leg against his chest. The carriage door slammed behind them. The man turned sideways to give his mother a narrow width of seating space, a sudden act of courtesy and chivalry. Men always seemed to be nice to his mother, even now. She pulled the boy onto her lap, clamping the suitcase and his rucksack between her legs. He was now able to look around. There were some twenty people in the enclosed space, some crying, some shaking, some trying to exchange information, some just staring downwards. There was a particular smell, more than the smell of sweat. He suddenly realised how hot he was and pulled off his winter coat. Outside, more people were trying to climb onto a wooden foot ledge, as they too tried to pull open the carriage door, but the man who had been so chivalrous to his mother had now appointed himself Guardian-of-the-Compartment and was warding off all invaders. The noise outside intensified, with shouting and pleading, with fists beating the carriage sides in increasingly futile despair, while the rattle of the machine guns was ever more continuous somewhere in the distance.

"We will throw them back; our soldiers will throw them back," promised a man in the corner of the compartment. Through the window, Jan could see a group trying to lift a grey mattress onto the roof of the train. Behind the mattress, the sky was becoming obscured by gun smoke. Just at that moment, the whole scene erupted in the biggest thump so far, with a simultaneous flash and crackling of flames, followed by an all-enveloping cloud of debris and dust which darkened the station, the train and the people left on the platform. During the aftermath of rumbling and shaking and more cries outside the window, the know-all commentator in the corner said, "They must have blown up the bridge; the bridge has gone; the town is cut off; it's their town now."

As if in a perfectly rehearsed and synchronised response to the blast, the train began to pull out of the station. While speed increased, there was a slithering sound from the roof above. The grey mattress fell past the window and two bodies fell with it. Karlovy Vary disappeared from view.

Within the compartment there was at first a long, tired silence. Then, those standing or sitting began tentative conversations. An elderly couple tried to open the compartment's inner door to the train corridor, where their family was located somewhere among people and possessions. The Guardian-Man now promoted himself to a further position of status, that of Compartment Leader. He offered information and advice. He was consoling.

"Now, don't worry, folks; Prague is not much more than a hundred kilometres away. We should be there within hours on this branch line system. In the meantime, remember that our army is the most mechanised in Europe; nothing can beat our Škoda equipment. Any German advance will be halted and reversed; you'll see. You'll all soon be home again. Try to rest. Look at how calm this little fellow and his mother are." He patted Jan on the head and leered at Ilona. "And if anyone needs the corridor toilets, first let me know and I'll clear the way for you."

After the initial burst of speed, the train now moved cautiously through open farmland. Often without apparent reason, there were long stops mid-line. The countryside looked peaceful.

"See what I told you," the Leader announced. "No Germans anywhere."

The others did not look too reassured. Ilona took a book from her handbag and offered to read a story, but Jan declined. He wanted to keep watch instead.

Slowly, the stop-start journey continued past rural Bohemian stations in which there were few signs of activity. After some four hours, the train moved even more slowly along a further branch track, there soon coming to an abrupt halt. They were among undulating fields. To one side lay woodland.

For the first time, windows and doors were thrown open. Along the length of the train, the compartments emptied as people jumped down to the ground to stretch their legs. Others slid down from their places on the roof. Many relieved themselves on the grass banks alongside the track or further away in the woods. The sun shone.

The man in the corner started complaining to the leader.

"You said that we would reach Prague within hours. So, where are we now then? Nowhere."

The leader re-emphasised certainty. "Don't worry; the driver needs a rest too, you know."

But as the afternoon passed and the train remained at a standstill, anxieties and rumours resurfaced, spreading down the corridors.

"The German and Czech armies must be fighting it out between us and Prague."

"The capital may soon be less safe than Karlovy Vary."

"We should turn back. Oh, what a situation."

There was renewed weeping.

The train waited till evening. Jan made friends with two other children in the compartment, a brother and sister whose parents had packed a game of draughts which, from time to time, became the centre of attention for everyone. Camaraderie was established. Those who had brought water and fruit and other provisions shared their bounty with the unprepared. With darkness, Jan fell asleep. His mother made a niche for him, padded with their coats, between two suitcases on the floor.

Next day, he woke to rolling movements and the sounds of voices. Trees were passing the window. A harsh outside daylight illuminated the muddle within. His mother, who was already awake, had been talking to a large woman, who now offered him bread and cheese with water. He ate and drank hungrily. The corner man, who continued to know everything, was complaining that this wasn't the route to Prague. As if to confirm his remarks, the train's brakes were slammed hard. A screeching halt threw bodies and belongings into further heaps.

Simultaneously, they all heard a new sound: a droning which intensified to an overhead roar, before momentarily ebbing away. Just as the familiar corner voice shouted, "A plane, maybe more," the sound started to return but as if with greater purpose. Almost immediately, Jan could now recognise the spluttering of machine gun fire as bullets smacked into the train roof to the accompaniment of shrieking and scrambling and slithering overhead. Outside the window, the sky was obscured by falling bodies, some in flat-out dives, some in contorted bundles. A half-opened head and a bloodied arm hung poised for a brief moment outside the top of the glazed carriage door, then a whole man fell past. The Compartment Leader now truly took command.

"Everyone to the floor. They'll be back again."

It wasn't easy. There were so many, up to three deep on the floor, as well as those double layered on the seating. As the planes came back and bullets ripped through the sides of the train and the doors, showering fragments of glass everywhere, the leader was the last to throw himself down, perhaps accidentally or deliberately, over Ilona, who in turn was shielding Jan beneath her.

Two planes left the sky. "Messerschmitts, Bf 109s," came the corner comment. No one answered. After a momentary lull throughout the train, there began a moaning and crying, punctuated by calls for assistance. Within the compartment, those among the human layers lying directly on the floor started pushing upwards. Those uppermost attempted to make room, trying to stand. Jan was aware that his mother was struggling to free herself. The upright ones above her were trying to help pull away the leader who, still lying on his stomach in a protective posture over Ilona, seemed incapable of disengagement. The leader's downwards-looking face was dripping a warm, sticky substance past Ilona onto Jan's upturned gaze two bodies below. The drips could not be avoided. Beyond his mother, he could see the leader's one visible eye looking unflinchingly straight at him.

"Please pull the man off," his mother was saying. The heaving above continued; the leader was a heavy man.

By the time Jan and Ilona were able to stand, Mr Know-It-All from the corner had already made a pronouncement: "Oh, he's dead alright." The discovery did not seem to displease him. He was in charge now.

"We must get his body off the train. There will be others."

Over the next hours, the train was left undisturbed. Jan was aware of a sense of purpose among the grown-ups. Broken glass was swept out with special brooms made from clothing wrapped around the walking sticks of the elderly. Any dead bodies still lying on the train roof were pulled off and thrown down the railway embankment, where they were buried in shallow graves dug by groups of the stronger men. The engine driver and his mate, both surprisingly unhurt, had found shovels. Teams of women moved from carriage to carriage, temporarily disinfecting and bandaging with the aid of torn shirts and some first aid boxes also supplied by the driver. A train committee had been formed, comprising the two drivers plus one representative from each carriage, a group which included Mr Know-It-All, who had managed to elevate himself still further, from Compartment Leader to full Carriage Chief.

Hunger now became the driving force behind all activity. The train committee agreed the need to move rapidly on to Prague, whatever the military situation.

2

IN THE EARLY evening of the day after leaving Karlovy Vary, the train at last slid into Prague. From the compartment windows, now mostly emptied of glass, the passengers leant outwards towards people on the crowded station platform.

"What station is this?" someone from the train called.

"Wilsonova," was the shout back.

"Are the Germans here? Is Beneš still in charge?"

The replies were reassuring. Relief spread everywhere. As yet, Prague was free.

The rest of that day remained hazy in Jan's memory. There was the confusion of people who were attempting to find each other among piles of unsorted luggage, some belonging to the dead. Medical orderlies were lifting the wounded onto stretchers, which were then manoeuvred through to the far end of the platform, beyond the archways, to ambulances waiting at exits guarded by khaki-uniformed soldiers.

Later, he recalled an onwards journey, in a car or taxi perhaps, which his mother and he shared with a large family and their various suitcases. The vehicle twisted through shadowy streets in the evening gloom. Soon afterwards, the driver said, "*Jilska Trida*," and halted. Then, he and his mother were standing alone on a pavement in a grey street of three- and four-storey terraced houses. Ilona was already knocking at a front door, which was opened by a white-haired woman who seemed to be expecting them. All three shook hands by the door. The woman said she was Madame Krchmenko. She was stooping, her body wrapped almost totally within a large, patterned apron. She led the way in, shuffling on furry slippers along a stone-flagged passageway. They followed her up two floors on a narrow staircase located in the centre of the house. There was the smell of lavatory at each floor landing. On the second-floor level, Madame K opened one of five doors.

"This is your room. There will be some soup in the kitchen in the basement when you are ready. The others have already eaten." She shuffled away.

They walked into the darker end of a small space. Near the door by which they had entered, a freestanding, carved wooden wardrobe and two plain chairs were randomly positioned. A frayed carpet covered the centre of the floor, which was boarded. Within the narrow wall which faced them, a central window opened to the street, across which lights were appearing. On one side of the window, parallel to the longer side walls of the room, was a bunk bed and on the other side, a single bed. A light bulb hung from the ceiling. His mother said, "Let's just leave our things, wash our hands, then go and have some nice soup."

Back on the landing at the head of the stairs, they saw an unmarked door which opened onto a small, windowless space. Inside, a WC pan faced the door and a washbasin had been angled into a corner. Each in turn tested these facilities, before walking together down to the ground floor, then further to the basement.

They were in a large kitchen many times the size of their own room. A pair of doors opened onto a yard, bounded by high, dark walls which rose to street level, above which Jan could see the stars. In the centre of the room, twelve assorted chairs surrounded a big, rectangular table. The steamy aroma of goulash soup filled the room.

On one side, Madame K was busy handling pots and pans and other utensils. She ladled large portions of soup into two bowls and invited her new guests to sit and eat. A loaf of bread and a plate of butter were ready on the table to accompany the soup. Jan was overjoyed. His hunger had seldom been so deliciously satisfied. After seeing her son's concentrated eating, Ilona also allowed herself to focus on the meal.

As they ate, with no time for conversation, another woman came into the kitchen. She was about Ilona's age, but of thin build with shiny, fair hair, smoothly brushed flat against her head and tied back in a bun. Jan noticed with some surprise that, like Madame K, this woman was also wearing a patterned apron and also walked in slippers. Madame K introduced her daughter Darja, who now began quietly to help her mother, her first task being to offer more soup and bread to these two new lodgers. Jan and Ilona accepted without hesitation. As he concentrated again on the taste of goulash soup, Jan decided that he very much liked Madame K and her daughter.

In the following weeks of October and November, the house on Jilska Street became home. Outside, a cold autumn turned into an even colder winter. Snow fell on Prague. The Vltava froze over. Inside, his mother transformed their room into a comfortable and familiar setting. From somewhere, she had managed to get woven materials to place over the beds for which Madame K had contributed extra blankets. A small table had appeared under the window and was soon covered with books and papers. The Krchmenkos had given Jan a collection of crayons and large sheets of white paper, on which he had drawn mountains, pine forests and his favourite animals, before pinning these works to one long side wall of the room, his contribution to the overall décor.

The house was full. At least twenty people were staying in various rooms on the upper floors. Common hardship reinforced everyone's sense of togetherness, even to the extent that most accepted each floor's shared toilet with its unique smells.

The house stayed warm. In the cellar next to the kitchen, a big old boiler burning coal and large logs was constantly tended by a gentleman friend of Darja's. This friend performed other household tasks which might otherwise have been carried out by an absent Monsieur K, about whose whereabouts there was uncertainty. The regular sounds of the boiler being stoked were reassuring, as was the gurgling and clanking of the house's hot water pipes.

The warmest place remained the kitchen, to which all were drawn and not only at mealtimes. Here, under clouds of steam drifting up from the cooker, Madame K and her daughter laboured endlessly to provide food for their lodgers.

Since Jan was the youngest resident, his elders tended to treat him as the house mascot. Two particular couples, the Bures and the Blaufelds, neighbours on the second-floor landing with his mother and himself, directly shared many conversations with him across the age divide. Herr and Frau Blaufeld, a small man and a large woman, were particularly kind. They regularly brought him a pair of *wurstchen mit senf*, long, succulent frankfurters with mustard and a helping of sauerkraut which they specifically fetched, even in the snow, from the kiosk at the Jilska corner junction with Vejvodova Street. He would often share this feast with two children from the third floor. These early teenagers tolerated Jan's younger years when they allowed him to join in their dramatic play-acting scenes performed on the house staircase and landings.

Sometimes, Jan's mother left the house without him on what she said were important things that he would find boring. On those occasions he would happily remain in the kitchen, where the Krchmenkos provided him with further drawing materials which Darja laid out across one end of the kitchen table. There, he would lose himself among his own colourfully imagined scenery, encouraged by Madame K and Darja, who would feed him sample selections of the lunch or supper in preparation.

Sometimes, Herr Blaufeld would come to the kitchen to admire Jan's drawings. Afterwards, he would say to his wife, "My dear, he is like the little boy we wanted to have."

One day when Ilona returned from 'an outing', she told him that soldiers from Germany were now living in the Karlovy Vary villa. He wondered whether any of the soldiers had tried his bedroom swing.

Throughout the early winter months, the residents continued to be drawn to the kitchen radio which brought the latest bulletins into the household. Every recent situation was followed, analysed at once, painfully debated. Only two days after Ilona and Jan's arrival, there had been news that President Beneš had resigned and that an army general was acting as interim leader. Within a few further days, the radio had carried Beneš's address to the nation, regretting the political situation, praising the Czech army.

One of the guests, Herr Kovar, who with his wife shared a room on the same landing as the Duseks, had become indignant. "He's getting out while he can. What's the use of his particular thanks to 'our courageous army'? It's all right for him. He won't be here, as we shall be, when the Germans arrive."

As if to corroborate Herr Kovar's pessimism, the kitchen listeners learnt in the last week of October that their President had flown to London and that numbers of his colleagues had flown with him to be a 'government in exile'.

Herr Blaufeld defended the President: "Beneš is a good man. He will continue the fight from England, I am sure."

Kitchen political gloom continued through November as more announcements told of Polish and Hungarian troop annexations of Czech borderlands. The lodgers' anger mixed with perplexity. "How could they? Our Slavonic cousins supporting the German cause? Only too eager to bite into us, are they? Don't they realise that they will be next?"

The lodgers' discussions continued at mealtimes, a never-ending background flow, of which Jan was only marginally aware as he concentrated, with appreciation, on the Krchmenkos' cooking.

The last day of November 1938 was Jan's sixth birthday. In the kitchen, a small gathering held a celebration by eating a special apple cake which Darja had baked. A low announcement on the ever-tuned radio caught the attention of the ever-listening Herr Kovar, who then interrupted the birthday event. "I'm sorry to intrude, but a new Czech President has just been elected. A sixty-two-year-old lawyer, Doktor Emil Hacha. Poor man, he has no chance."

On that occasion, the other well-wishers held back their own comments.

Twice weekly throughout November and then into December, by which time temperatures had dropped to minus twenty degrees centigrade, Jan looked forward to special afternoon explorations with his mother, which always led to Wenceslas Square. They would arrive at the lowest end of the square in the north-west, by the office and insurance company buildings. Jan would immediately run uphill, ahead of his mother, past trams, cafés, hotels and shops, towards the statue of Saint Wenceslas on his horse, backed by the dominating mass of the National Museum. On one occasion, when snow was falling more heavily than usual, his mother took him to the cinema just east of Wenceslas's statue, where he saw his first film, *Snow White and the Seven Dwarfs*. When the witch initially appeared, Jan dived under his seat. For days afterwards, he wondered if she was connected to that first witch in his life. Usually, however, the purpose of their visits led mother and son straight up the central incline to rows of wooden trellis tables covered with wooden boxes, all laid out across the cobblestones over the narrow width of the square. At the ends of each row stood groups of police who were watching people walking slowly along the lines of tables and peering into the boxes which contained hundreds of envelopes. Here were letters from soldiers on active service, written from locations censored from the receiver to destinations in Prague unknown to the sender. Here, links could be made: the trellis rows were arranged alphabetically by addressees' surnames, from A, by Wenceslas high up on the slope, to Z, by the insurance companies at the bottom.

The boy would always get to row D ahead of his mother. There, he would wait for her to catch up because he was not tall enough to reach the boxes at the back of the tables. When she began her careful check, envelope by envelope, he was impatient. About once every two weeks, they would be lucky. They would find an envelope addressed in his father's broad handwriting to 'ILONA' and 'JAN DUSEK. PRAGUE'. Nothing more. Then, they would take the envelope quickly past the policemen to their favourite café on the west slope, where chess was always being played in ideal silence and concentration. The gummed labels would be slit open and the letter inside examined word by word, his mother reading several times over during his slower single read. Everyone's envelopes had always already been opened and resealed. Sometimes, words or sentences, or even whole paragraphs, had been blocked out. In their case, the remaining text was mostly the same, his father hoping that they were well, repeating that he was well, that they were not to worry, that they all would be together again soon. Finally, he sent his love, and he would write again.

Ilona always placed such a letter within its envelope carefully into her handbag. She would drink her coffee slowly and gaze out onto the square while Jan concentrated on an adjacent table's game of chess, wondering about the short-term movements of the little wooden pawns, the grand sweeps of the crowned queen, the single slides of the sheltered old king. The chess players took no notice of the boy. After one of the players announced, "*Mat*," and the losing king was laid flat on the board, then it would be time to return to Jilska Street.

In the evenings after such 'Wenceslas Days', when Jan and Ilona were in their room together, the son drawing, the mother reading or writing letters, they would pause to talk about his father. They wondered about the location of his unit, about the date of his possible return. In these conversations, Ilona would always be positive, always optimistic, perhaps on her son's behalf.

The December snow continued to fall and with the snow came Christmas. In spite of troubling news bulletins on the kitchen radio, which reported military skirmishes at borders east, west and south and civilian skirmishes in the cities of Brno and Bratislava, the Krchmenkos and their lodgers were determined to celebrate. Personal religious variations were no obstacle; everyone was a part of the festivities.

Early on Christmas Eve, there was a knocking at the front door of the house. Madame K called Jan, who was drawing in the kitchen, to help open the door latches. Outside on the street, a very large bear was stomping his big feet, causing a rattle of the chains which were wrapped around his ankles. Jan did not like the chains.

The bear snorted into the cold air and growled, "Have you been a good boy?"

Jan did not answer. Firstly, he was not sure that he had been a good boy and, secondly, the bear's chains continued to disturb him. A man, who had been leading the bear from door to door, pulled a ball from a sack and offered it to Jan.

"You've said nothing, but you're probably good, so you can have your present anyway..."

Jan turned back into the house without taking the ball. He thought that the man's voice sounded growling, like the bear's.

Later, the whole household assembled in the kitchen. Madame K and Darja, both in festive clothing, having shed their patterned aprons, introduced Darja's friend Jiri to the lodgers. A brightly decorated Christmas tree filled the far corner of the room and stretched to the ceiling. Madame K guided Jan to the tree, from which she handed him a wrapped present.

"*Veselé Vánoce*," she said as she gave him a clumsy kiss. Then, as Jiri switched off the room lights, Darja simultaneously lit candles on the kitchen table. Alongside the dancing flames, the meal began with a sauerkraut soup, *kapustnica*, ladled with smoked sausage and sour cream from a large tureen at the table's centre. Then, Madame K brought forwards silver salvers, on which she had arranged four giant carp, each decorated with rings of roast chestnuts and lemon slices. There were accompanying dishes of buttered potatoes and puréed red cabbage with apple, or, if guests preferred, alternative potato salads with carrot and pickle. All ate with gusto, boosted by wine or Pilsner or merely water. An enthusiastic few ventured further to the desserts, for choices of Czechish poppy-seed dumplings or Germanic *apfelstrudel* with cream. A finale of plum liqueurs ushered in speeches and toasts to the Krchmenkos, who were red-faced, this time not so much from cooking but from the praise lavished upon them.

There was still time for everyone to exchange small presents before joining in the clearing-up. Then the whole party, of varied beliefs or of none, came together to make the short march through the snow for midnight mass at the nearby church of St Giles on Zleth Street. Madame K was heavily wrapped and leaning on her daughter's arm.

In the early new year months of 1939, Jan began morning sessions at a nearby kindergarten. The school was filled with the children of local townspeople, joined by those from the many new families who had flooded into Prague as refugees. Jan was glad to make friends of his own age. The school regime was strict, even for six-year-olds, so that by lunchtime he was always ready for the arrival of his mother with their picnic. They would find a bench in a small square and would sit, wrapped up, eating hungrily and watching passers-by coping with the snow. After lunch they would become explorers, their routes taking them daily in new directions, either within the Old or New Towns or into the Jewish Quarter or, via the Little Quarter, up the hillside to the Castle and Hradčany. Their walks took them under vaulted arcades, past gates to secret courtyards, alongside the Vltava's bank and over her bridges, or high into vineyard terraces for views over the city. At times his mother would try to move him forwards more quickly, as when he would become rooted in front of the town hall's astronomical clock, waiting patiently for the hourly strike to usher out the skeleton of Death, the procession of the eleven Apostles, plus St Paul and St Peter. At another time, in the Strahov monastery, they would be unable to continue their tour because Jan would want to play endlessly with the rotating mediaeval bookstand. Only at lengthy afternoon recitals in the Municipal House would he be ready to move away early, this time impatiently, ahead of Ilona, who was still enjoying the music.

In the second week of February, the snow still lay thick on the ground. Jan's routine had continued with regularity: mornings in the kindergarten, afternoon walks in the city, noisy evenings in the K's kitchen and, later, sleep in the small, quiet room. It was on a Friday lunchtime when the world changed again. He and a friend were running out of the school building towards the outer courtyard walls, their coats unbuttoned, each child searching for the familiar face beyond the school gates. Then he saw them together, his father with an arm around his mother's shoulders, their free arms waving towards him. His father was smiling; his mother was laughing. Jan hurled himself at both his parents. His father scooped him up and also managed, with the same sweeping movement, to lift Ilona into the air. All three were still clinging together outside the school gates well after the remaining parents and children had dispersed.

That evening, before supper in the Krchmenkos' kitchen, Ivan was introduced to the assembled household and at once became the target of questioning. What had been happening at the front? Had there been a battle? What now? Was Prague safe? His answers were short, direct and quiet.

"Yes, there has been fighting, particularly around Plzen, which remains in Czech hands, but probably not for much longer. A new German spring offensive, backed by their superior air power, is expected to begin in March. Our own armed forces are well-trained, well-equipped and ready to fight. We also have Škoda tanks which are better than any German armour. But President Hacha has ordered that we offer no resistance. Instead, there is to be a general withdrawal. My own reservist unit, among others, has been disbanded. Soon all will be over. And so, no, there is no hope for Prague."

When the meal began, there was a general concentration on eating. No one looked around to see who might be the most upset. All went to bed early.

The room on the second floor now held the family of three. His mother and father slept on the bunk bed, his father below, his mother on top. His parents would be talking in low voices as he fell asleep, easily as ever. Sometimes in the night, when he turned over in a dream, he thought that they were still talking. Once he found himself half awake, hearing his father saying, "But I'm still a member of our National Socialist Party; they will have me on their lists."

A week later, an official-looking envelope with a Monte Carlo postmark arrived for his mother, who at first read her letter alone. Then, with drooping shoulders, she shared the news with her husband, who held her as she began to cry. In her tears she turned to Jan to tell him that his grandmother had died. For some seconds, the boy would not accept what he had heard, then, seeing Ilona's shrunken figure, he gave way to his first great grief and began to weep uncontrollably with her.

By midday, Ilona had recovered enough to make plans. "I'll get down there, even if we have to lose some of our last money. There should still be trains. After all, France is not at war."

Within two days, she was gone, and within seven days, she had returned. To her husband and son she recounted details of her journey, of the cremation on the Monte Carlo hillside and of the cask within a stone wall niche, facing the Mediterranean. Only years later did Ilona explain to Jan that his grandmother had ended her own life. "She left a note to say that she did not want to be a burden to us in such difficult times."

On the first day of March, the people of Prague woke to see the skies white with flurrying shapes, all larger than familiar snowflakes. Jan ran into the street and brought one of the fallen sheets of paper up to his parents. The leaflet was from the enemy. His father read out the wording:

"To the citizens of Bohemia and Moravia. Your President Beneš, your Government, your Communist Party, your Russian supporters, have together pushed the Czech people to war. Capitulate now to prevent terrible bloodshed. The German High Command is today initiating 'Operation Spring Awakening'."

Over the following days, all radio and press war items were confusing and contradictory. There was talk of ill-equipped invaders suffering large-scale frostbite. No one seemed to be sure what would happen next. Perhaps the French and the British would, after all, back up their promises of support? Then, on 10th March, listeners learnt that Doctor Hacha had been summoned to Berlin.

"No choice, you see," Herr Kovar reminded the kitchen group. "Poor little weakling Hacha. With his heart condition, he'll do everything that Hitler wants."

The lodgers continued to visit the kitchen daily at all times. From 12th March, they started to become aware that broadcasts from Germany included press statements which told of assaults by Czech nationals on peaceful Germans in Bohemia.

"Typical rubbish," Herr Kovar interrupted "Their lies are deliberately working up aggression in the streets."

An announcement on 13th March prompted Herr Blaufeld to hurry up the stairs to relay information to his wife, who was resting.

"My dear, President Hacha is on his way to Berlin. Hopefully he will be negotiating with Herr Hitler and Field Marshal Göring. There will surely be an amicable agreement. All cannot be lost."

Frau Blaufeld could be heard weeping.

At breakfast on 14th March, the whole household, less Frau Blaufeld who had taken more permanently to her bed, heard Prague radio announcing that at 4.30am that morning, President Hacha had signed the document which declared the Czech provinces of Bohemia and Moravia were to be 'protectorates' of the German Reich.

"The Czech army has been ordered to 'stand down'. At 6.00am, fourteen divisions of the Wehrmacht, some

two hundred thousand men, have begun to cross the
latest re-established borders and are moving towards
Prague."

Jan, sleeping huddled in his bed early on the morning of
15th March, felt a shoulder being shaken. The room was
still dark. His father, standing over him, whispered, "Put on
your clothes, your mother is asleep, come, we are going out
together."

Ivan helped his son to dress more quickly and wrote a
note for his wife. Then, the two quietly left the house.

The sky was a dense grey. The last of the winter snows had
fallen in the night and lay still frozen on the pavements. There
were few people on Jilska Street, but the kiosk at Vejvodova
Street was already open, with heat rising from an urn of
simmering water. They joined a small queue to buy *wirstchen
mit senf* and rolls with sauerkraut, which they continued to
eat as they walked on past the Bethlehem Chapel towards
the Vltava, before turning northwards along the riverbank to
the Charles Bridge, Ivan's chosen destination. There, by the
Old Town Bridge Tower, they joined a fast-growing crowd
which was lining the surrounding pavements and filling the
adjacent Křižovnické Square. People were of all ages, heavily
covered in winter clothing, men with peaked caps, children
with balaclavas. There was much restless movement, with
warmth being gathered in closeness with others. Ripples of
news were exchanged. A man next to Ivan muttered, "That
Hacha has signed away our country. Now they are coming."

A few snowflakes continued to settle as the sky lightened.
Everyone's attention was becoming focused across the bridge,

its bordering lines of guardian saints directing gazes to the Vltava's western bank and the spire of St Nicholas Church beyond. A general rumbling of uncertain origin floated across the water, perhaps a combination of voices and the sounds of vehicle engines rising somewhere below Prague Castle. Soon, there was no more reason for uncertainty. As the first motorcycle troop turned the Mala Strana Square bend to reach the west bank, the watchers grew silent. The advancing column, snow- and mud-covered, moved slowly onto and across the bridge. First came pairs of parallel riders, steel-helmeted, in full battle dress with rifles shouldered over greatcoats. Neither rider looked left or right. A further column followed, this time with similarly equipped single riders and sidebar passengers. Behind the motorcyclists there followed what seemed to be an unending column of open trucks, each vehicle filled with seated helmeted troops but with a single gunner standing by each tailboard next to a machine gun, its barrel pointing to the sky, its bullet belts hanging and swaying loosely. Some of the seated men waved uncertainly to the onlookers, who did not respond. Then came lines of tarpaulin-covered lorries with hidden loads, each lorry with armed soldiers again guarding the tailboards. Larger lorries followed, each towing heavy field guns on muddy wheels, every gun escorted by marching infantrymen. Behind the guns stretched a seemingly endless line of foot soldiers, three abreast, this time with rifles at the slope, the men in rhythmic step to the sharp commands of, "*Links, rechts, links, rechts*," a continuous khaki colour flooding out of the background of the Little Quarter and overwhelming the length of Charles Bridge, alongside the stone saints of history. On and on swept the flood, now with officers marching beside every twentieth line of troops, past the shuffling, sullen, silent spectators, each of whom could at any one moment have taken fists out of pockets and leant forwards to make contact with a helmet, a face or a uniformed chest. But all held back.

It was then that the main reason for the rumbling became apparent. As the first tank swung into view beyond the west side of the water, the crowd took in a single communal breath which was held for a moment. Then, a thousand untimed exhalations followed as the leading tank's tracks slithered onto the bridge. There followed the slow, forward momentum of tank after tank, mechanical beasts rumbling and slithering into Prague, a continuous and unstoppable process.

Only after Jan claimed hunger did his father relent from his own watchful stance. The pair were about to move away when, following in the wake of the very last tank, a third group of motorcyclists ushered a fleet of large and shiny open-topped black cars over the bridge. These cars were chauffeured. In the rear of the first vehicles sat men in khaki, with hard flat caps and many ribbons on their chests. Two last cars followed, their blackness complemented by the equally black, shiny and medalled uniforms of their passengers, two per car, looking with ease and confidence at the scenes around them. The sight of four such arrogant faces finally broke the watchers' silence, which gave way to outbursts of muttered curses and even shouting and fist waving from those who were still brave enough.

As Jan was pulling his father away, a new tremor swept through the onlookers, with voices further raised and arms pointing westwards. Over Prague Castle, a flag was being raised. "The swastika flag," his father said. It was a sign for the crowd to disperse. The snowflakes were turning into rain.

That evening, the kitchen meal began at its most subdued. With the exception of Ivan and Jan, none of the lodgers had ventured out of the house during the day, so Ivan briefly described the scenes at the Charles Bridge. All listened without interrupting.

The first comment came from Madame Krchmenko, still standing by the side of her cooker. In a slow voice, she said that Darja had been in the city during the afternoon. "Such scenes she saw and heard. There were loudspeakers asking people to come out onto the streets. 'This should be a day of welcoming,' the loudspeaker voices said. As pavements began to fill up, German troops with revolvers in their belts began to line the pavement frontages. In case of unrest, do you think? Then, Darja said there was more parading… groups of German soldiers were carrying small Czech children who held bunches of flowers in their arms, and there were more soldiers arm in arm with young Czech women in our national dress. Then, crowds gathering in late afternoon, with people raising their arms in the Nazi salute as more troops marched past. Darja was shocked. Well-dressed people saluting, women with hats, gloves and handbags. Disgusting. My daughter says she even saw one woman saluting with her right arm while drying her weeping eyes with her left hand. Having it both ways, she was. Then all became worse, with white horses pulling carts filled with more children and flowers, all just in front of riders on three white horses leading *his* car…

yes, *he* had arrived, saluting like a puppet to left and right. Bastard. He will be in Prague Castle tonight, that man, now in the home of the Kings of Bavaria."

It was not long before the lodgers filed up to their rooms.

On the following morning of 16th March, a usually wordy kitchen radio began to blare out military music. Chords of appropriate pomp were followed by an announcement that *'The Protectorate of Bohemia and Moravia has been established'*. As the address developed into an ever higher-pitched lecturing mode, Madame Krchmenko moved purposefully over the kitchen floor and, for the first time in the lodgers' memories, switched off the programme. Back among her familiar kitchen utensils, she was heard muttering, "Protectorate indeed... prison state more likely... go home, why do you not go home?"

For the rest of March and into early April, the whole of Prague was waiting for more to happen, but the days remained outwardly undisturbed. The mass of German troops stayed in barracks outside the city. Posters in the streets informed the public that a German infantry general had 'taken over command' of Prague and that Czech and German police shared responsibility for order. Radio bulletins from Prague or Berlin were calming and optimistic, with commentators denouncing foreign apprehension.

Occupation events were much discussed by the lodgers. Herr Blaufeld found himself becoming the most informed, most worried assessor of 'The Situation'. From the news stalls, he would bring back daily publications. He would then analyse opinion and statistics to relay essential information to the household. "We are guessing," he would say, "for remember, it's the Germans who now control our press. Much is kept from us. Prague is full of rumours. There are collaborators and informers everywhere. It is said that thousands have been arrested on the invaders' and even on Hacha's orders. There are stories of night-time visits by the Gestapo and the SS to certain city homes, of people being taken away, of their ashes being returned to their families in small wooden boxes. But one surely cannot believe that?"

The lodgers' private worries were only privately discussed. Intimations were exchanged about finance, which was running out. The future was so uncertain.

For Jan, those first weeks of occupation were surprisingly happy. April brought in the spring air to rival any remaining snow eddies. Morning kindergarten continued. Trees were beginning to bud around the school playground. The scent of early lilac in the courtyard drifted through open classroom windows. His mother and father were both now usually outside the school gates at lunchtime to meet him. It appeared that his parents had sometimes been together all morning in various 'offices'. Other words like 'solicitor' and 'consulate' were new to him.

The favourite afternoon walks also continued, often more adventurously when his father made up a trio. Ivan was at all times cheerful in the company of his wife and son. He would hoist the boy onto his shoulders and stride through the streets, humming the march from Aida, which he explained he had seen at La Scala in Milan, when elephants and camels had processed across the stage. Sometimes Ivan would laughingly also lift his wife into the air and twirl her round in a circle, exclaiming, "My Ilona, my little Ilona," a movement which Ilona did not resist.

At times, Ivan and Jan would walk together. On one such walk, an incident happened which would remain in Jan's memory longer and more clearly than many later and more outwardly important events in his life. He and his father were walking up the east side of Perlova Street on their way into the Old Town. The afternoon sun was casting deep shadows on the opposite house frontages, while their own street side was filled with light. Father and son walked in parallel on the narrow pavement. The street was almost empty. Suddenly approaching them, on the same pavement but from the opposite direction, was a single Gestapo officer, perfectly dressed in his black uniform and gleaming boots, the brim of his peaked cap equally shiny over blue eyes and cropped blond hair. As they approached each other, the boy suddenly knew that three people could not remain side by side on this pavement width. His father was continuing to walk straight onwards, as was the oncoming officer. Then, perhaps two seconds before collision, it was the uniformed man who stepped down into the gutter which separated roadway from pavement kerbstone. In the act of stepping down, he swung his upper torso fully sideways towards the pair on the pavement, simultaneously saluting them and smiling, the sun glinting on leather and silver studs. Once he had fully passed, he then again stepped up onto the pavement. Years after, perhaps when needing to narrow his shoulder span in a crowd, Jan as a young man would practise the same sideways movement, that swivel both of recognition and of power, the gesture of the strong towards the weak. On that day in the

Prague afternoon, Ivan had said nothing but had continued to walk forwards steadily with his son.

At the beginning of May, Jan fell in love. His mother had planned a country picnic. She had befriended a Madame Novotna, whose daughter Naďa had begun to play with Jan in the kindergarten. On a Saturday morning, the two mothers and their children took a local bus northwards out of the city towards Veltrusy, a nearby country town from which a further walk soon brought them into the most rural of landscapes.

The air was balmy. Before them, the land swept past farmsteads towards distant hills. Alongside wooden barns, lilac bushes swayed in disorganised formations of purple and white. Further on, a long, gradual downwards slope led to an apple orchard bursting with blossom. The two children ran towards this magnet of colour, before throwing themselves onto meadow grass below the branches of the apple trees. The mothers followed slowly, talking of worldly events. They sensed that the children were in their own world.

On the grass, Jan found himself noticing Naďa, seeing her as he had not seen her before. The sunlight, filtering through the waving branches over her head, made patterns of shadows on her face. She had dark brown eyes. He wanted to kiss her. Instead, he bent round to tear up a handful of grass, which he threw at her, laughing. She, by contrast, became serious and lay there, studying him. There were strands of grass in her hair and on her shoulders. Her eyes were so large. He wanted always to be with her.

That night in his bed, he lay wide awake for a long time, thinking about the time under the trees, the picnic which had followed, the intervals between running and playing, he trying to be less boisterous, she trying to be less serious, he wishing the day would never end.

His recollections continued so intensely that he was hardly aware of his parents talking quietly on their side of the window. He would eventually have fallen asleep, but the house was suddenly shaken by a loud and continuous knocking at the front door. At first, he remembered the Christmas bear; there had been loud knocking then. But this was spring, not Christmas. What was happening?

Doors were opening. He could hear voices, Madame K's among them. His parents were now on their feet; his father had slipped on a pair of trousers and a pullover; his mother was in her dressing gown. His father said, "Stay here, please," and walked out onto the landing. The staircase lights were on. The voices were becoming louder, among them men's voices giving orders. There were heavy steps on the stairs and shouts of, "*Heraus, heraus, alle heraus!*" There was the sound of wood being smashed.

His father came back into the room. To Ilona, he said, "They are not Gestapo; they are the SS." To Jan, he said, "Wrap a coat around yourself, my son." Together, all three went onto the landing.

Two black-uniformed and booted SS men, their red, white and black swastika armbands jumping out in the dim light, were positioning the other lodgers against the walls. A third man, in officer uniform, was facing inward to Herr and Frau Blaufelds' room, the broken door of which was partly hanging from one hinge. "*Heraus, 'raus, schnell, schnell,*" he barked.

Frau Blaufeld appeared, filling her doorway, shaking and tearful in her dressing gown, just as Madame K, also in a dressing gown, came up the stairs holding some papers.

Twelve people now filled the landing space. On the perimeter, against walls and doors, stood Jan and his parents, Herr and Frau Bures, Herr and Frau Kovar and Frau Blaufeld. In the centre, under a flowery lampshade, were the three Gestapo officers and Madame K. The officer who had broken down the Blaufelds' door was now studying one of Madame K's papers.

"Floor Two, nine people listed, we have eight here. One missing." After more checking of the paper. "…So, where is Herr Blaufeld?"

A frozen moment. Shuffling and trembling. No one spoke. The SS leader waited, somewhat deliberately tapping the toe of his right boot on the wooden floor. It was then that the assembled group became aware of the most pungent smell which, to the regular dwellers on the landing, was on the one hand the familiar and acceptable smell of human excrement but which now, on the other hand, was such an intensification of that smell that its source had become obvious. The SS leader's nose now answered his own question. One step took him to the landing toilet door, which he found to be locked. His fist pounded the door. "*Aufmachen, aufmachen!*"

As Jan wondered if the man would use his boot, there was the faintest click from inside the toilet. Mr SS pulled the door outwards.

More frozen moments. Those on the landing looked into the darkened space. The small figure of Herr

Blaufeld, almost half the size of his wife, was sitting, as if cemented forever to the pan, his head and shoulders bowed downwards, his body trembling, his thin, knobbly knees exposed, his pyjama trousers wrapped around his ankles. The smell swirled around the landing. Jan's eyes, which were at the level of Herr B's head, tried unsuccessfully to make supportive contact. Frau B moved in agitation towards her husband, but she was swept back by the Gestapo leader, who now broke the lull.

"*Wischen sie ihren hintern und stehen sie auf.*" Wipe your bum and get up, he said in a level voice.

Everything ended quickly. Herr B came out of his retreat. He did what was asked of him, perhaps his last noble moment. Coats were found for him and for Frau B. They were together now. They went downstairs between their captors, Madame K trailing behind. The front door banged shut. Outside, the roar of an engine soon faded.

On the landing, the remaining lodgers touched each other in hesitation. Jan's father guided his wife and son back into their own room. Behind the closed door, they embraced in the darkness. Ilona was shuddering.

Next morning, Jan asked his parents why the men in black had taken away Herr and Frau Blaufeld.

"What have they done? When will they come back?" His mother's and father's answers were vague, unsatisfactory; they wanted him to feel secure.

The impact of the night-time visit permanently changed the mood of the house. The lodgers were now more reserved with each other. When they were not out in the city on errands or visits, they remained for longer periods of time in their own rooms. Social life in the kitchen diminished. Mealtimes were less discursive. Personal opinions or reactions to news bulletins were self-censored. Beyond mealtimes, only Jan continued to be the constant visitor to the kitchen, energetically sketching at the kitchen table, regularly tasting samples of the K's culinary output, much to the joy of the cooks.

By late May, the early summer heat of central Europe had reached Prague. In the Duseks' room at night, the small window and closed door combined to give little ventilation. At night-time, when the window was left as fully open to the street as possible, an invasion of mosquitoes would begin. The mosquitoes liked Jan. He would lie on his back and wait, his arms and hands free on the outside of the sheets because of the heat. An attack was always heralded by the whining sound of a mosquito diving… eeeyaoowoo-uh! Silence, the moment of the creature's arrival on his body, almost the same moment as the puncture, the sucking of blood from ears, face, neck, arms or hands. He knew that if he could anticipate the exact end of the flight then he could smack the mosquito dead at the split second of its landing. He became a killer. Sometimes a second or third mosquito was already whining its way out of the darkness. More numbers meant more victories, more kills; one smack could deal multiple deaths. Jan enjoyed these skirmishes, the pitting of his wits against the instincts of the flying creatures. Inevitably he fell asleep during battles, allowing his opponents to gain the advantage. In the morning, he would try to find and count up squashed mosquito bodies, while Ilona rubbed soap over his wounds.

One lunchtime in early June, he found his mother waiting alone outside the school gates. She told him that his father was resting.

"He didn't sleep well last night; it was so hot."

They postponed the afternoon's exploration and returned to the house. In the hallway, Madame K met them to say that a doctor was upstairs with Dr Dusek. They hurried up to find the two men talking. His father was still lying on the lower bunk level while the visiting doctor was sitting on Jan's bed. He stood up.

"Frau Doktor Dusek, your husband has angina pectoris; he has had a small heart attack, probably the result of anxiety, fatty foods, smoking, many things. I have prescribed appropriate medication and am advising rest, as much rest as possible. Please make contact if you need me." He shook hands formally with father, mother and son before leaving.

Once again, their pattern of life shifted. His father continued to dress in the morning but often rested, spending more time horizontally than vertically. Ilona brought him books from the library, including biographies of particular philosophers. Sometimes, in the evenings, when Jan heard his father and mother talking about the books, he would try to understand what his father was saying.

"Over so much time, lying here, I've tried to reread some Kant, Hegel, Schopenhauer and Nietzsche in their published sequence. What advice do they give us? I hold to Kant; he is my man. He is liberal, his political philosophy appeals to the heart, he is one for freedom. He says, 'There can be nothing more dreadful than that the actions of a man should be subject to the will of another.' His belief that every man is 'an end in himself' has led to the American doctrine of the Rights of Man, to democracy. I like Schopenhauer too; in some ways he followed in Kant's footsteps, believing in reason and rationality rather than emotion, valuing peace rather than war. Pity that he had such a low opinion of women, apparently because he disliked his mother. Hegel, I find difficult. He thought that each of us should support only our own background and country, even if that meant fighting a war which would then be acceptable and not an 'evil'. I can't agree. Wouldn't it be best for all of us to be citizens of one world? Nietzsche always worried me the most and still does. He is so dangerous. He dismisses rationality, promotes emotion, direct, violent, unhindered by thought. So, ruthlessness and war are acceptable to him as long as they are carried out by 'great men', by 'aristocratic' leaders. He liked Napoleon. He doted, at least for a while, on Wagner, as I guess so many still do for different reasons. Nietzsche would have admired Wagner's superman Siegfried, sword in hand, battling against the Niebelungen. He would have believed in such a hero. Hitler has been able to latch on to and make use of such a myth… ugh… heroes can be so deluded." His father's words would be the slide into sleep… into thick, green jungle plants called Niebelungen being swished by mighty, gleaming swords…

Ivan continued to maintain his daily outward calm equilibrium and sense of humour. He gave chess lessons to the boy so that Jan would begin to understand the tournaments in the Wenceslas Square café. He joined the kitchen meals but ate lightly. He seldom left the house but instead had long discussions with his wife before Ilona went out with a programme of mutually agreed tasks.

Ilona now had to become leader of the family. She began to take Jan on her journeys into the city, expeditions which sometimes took place in mornings as well as afternoons so that he began to miss kindergarten. No longer did such outings just explore areas of the city but also took the pair into big buildings, each often with long entrance steps, high porticos and wide doorways, many guarded by Czech policemen or German soldiers. Ilona and Jan would go to a desk where his mother would make an enquiry and then, if they were not turned away at once, there would follow a waiting room – often full of people – and sometimes, though rarely, an onward route to a bigger office where another man behind another desk would ask his mother questions, would look at papers and keep copies and always, as they left, she would seem disappointed.

In the first week of July, the kindergarten closed for the summer. Ivan was slowly recovering strength and was going out to the doctor's surgery for tests. Once again, he and Jan were able to walk together by the river. The boy was happy that his father was beginning to hum arias from his favourite operas, to point out special places, even to ask riddles.

On each weekday morning of the month, Ilona now started to take Jan regularly to a large, stone building, many storeys high, in the centre of the city.

"It is the consulate building," she explained. "Where people are given permission to go to other countries. Your father and I would like to take you to other parts of the world. To do this we need to have important papers called exit visas. These are difficult to obtain but you and I will succeed." Jan felt pride in being his mother's assistant on such an important task.

Each day they would arrive early, Ilona carrying documents in a borrowed briefcase, Jan with his rucksack holding their lunch picnic and some of his toys.

On any morning, however early, a queue had already formed. Perhaps some people had been there all night. All through each day, the queue continued to lengthen because new arrivals always outnumbered those who were leaving.

This pattern continued throughout July. Sometimes the queue moved faster, sometimes there were long delays. Sometimes those who joined late would find themselves near the entrance steps because the queue before them stretched all the way around two city blocks before returning. Those at the back continued to wait patiently; there was no alternative. Jan fashioned new delights out of the process. While grown-ups kept their places, he and other children from the queue, his new friends, would run races around one or more blocks. The Czech policemen who were in charge of the queue appeared to tolerate the children's wilder ways. Race champions would receive prizes from family packets, fruit, perhaps, or special lumps of cheese or even chocolate. Groups of children formed and reformed together to play and to talk, often finding out much about each other and their respective family plans. One such queuing friend, a girl called Rachel, spoke excitedly about her parents' and grandparents' proposals to take her to Israel.

Each day, after some eight hours of waiting, the consulate's great double entrance doors would be closed and the queue ordered to disperse. Each night, Ilona would relay more disappointment to her husband.

One morning at the start of August, Jan and his mother again left his father on his bed and arrived early at the consulate headquarters. The queue was already forming but seemed shorter than usual. The sun had not yet risen, and the air was so cool that multiple waiting breaths clouded the stone walls of the building. Jan recognised familiar faces who, like his mother and himself, were returning day after day with determined purpose. Greetings were exchanged. He went to search for a friend with whom he could play. Perhaps Rachel would be there, but no sooner had he run off than he heard his mother calling him back. The policemen were ordering everyone to move along faster. This was unusual. What was happening around the block at the front entrance? Were people being turned away?

Something was certainly different that day. Over the next five hours, there was a continuous forward tide of movement so that by early afternoon, Ilona and her son found themselves for the first time standing at the foot of the broad flight of steps which rose upwards under a high canopy towards the main entrance. There was no pausing. Guards in brown uniforms ushered them up, past sentries at attention by the imposing front doors, then through at last.

In a large lobby area, two men in black uniforms, behind yet another table, were arranging long lists of names.

"Are they Gestapo or SS?" Jan whispered to his mother. Ilona shushed her son.

The forms which she took from her briefcase were checked against the table lists, but this time, all was brief formality. They were moved almost at once through a further opening, now to stand uncertainly within a three-storey high entrance hall, at the centre of which a staircase, wide as a large room, stretched up to a main first floor. High over the stairs, a domed glass roof filtered light over hanging flags of the kind his father so disliked. Again, they did not wait long. A new guard stepped forwards to become their personal escort. He led them up the main stairs, heavily balustered, thickly carpeted. No one else followed behind. On the first floor, the escort moved past a series of double doors before he indicated a stop by the widest doors of all. Jan fidgeted. Ilona was motionless, staring at the wood grain in front of her face. The escort knocked. A voice called, "*Herein.*" Again they moved forwards, inwards.

The room was large. Behind a desk, deeper and longer than Madame Krchmenko's kitchen table, sat a bald-headed SS officer. His face and neck were heavily wrinkled. Above him, framed in gold, hung a full-length portrait of Hitler, looking stern. High windows flanked each side of the Führer. The officer waved the escort away, the man closing the doors quietly. Another wave indicated two leather armchairs in front of the desk. "*Bitte sitzen sie beide.*"

Jan wriggled into his chair which comfortably engulfed him. Ilona sat forwards carefully. She wore a light green dress, her dark hair piled up. Leaning towards her, the officer continued to talk in his native German mother tongue.

"Frau Doktor Dusek, I have studied your papers." He tapped the desk. "I understand that Doktor Dusek is indisposed, for which my condolences. I see that he and you have made an application to travel with your son to the United States of America, via England. Please, why is this? I am interested in your reasons. Surely, we have so much to offer you here? And you, of course, have so much to offer us. Your papers," he tapped the desk a second time, "and your backgrounds all indicate your excellent potential contribution to the new Reich. Your surgery in Carlsbad," he did not use the Czech word, Karlovy Vary, "is waiting for your husband's and your own early return to work. You will be welcomed back. Your assistants are merely keeping everything in order on your behalf and, of course, on the Führer's behalf. The Sudetenland is now peaceful under his leadership." He leant back, straightening his shoulders. Over his head, the Führer's portrait appeared to approve, to encourage further rhetoric. "The Czechs are now part of a stronger Protectorate which your husband, as a postgraduate of Prague University, will no doubt wish actively to support." He sat up, even more upright. "And I would like to add, Frau Doktor, that the Reich and Protectorate would not only suffer from the loss of your undoubted joint professional talents but that your community in Carlsbad would lose from its midst," he paused, "a woman of exceptional... how might one express it... presentability." He seemed pleased with his last choice of word.

Jan looked sideways at his mother. It was her turn. Ilona kept to her self-allotted role. She blushed slightly. "*Danke, Herr Major,*" she began. "Firstly, thank you for your condolences for my husband's health. Fortunately, he is becoming stronger. I know that he, like myself, appreciates the far-reaching events which have recently taken place in Europe, as well as the opportunities and challenges now open to so many of us. He and I have spoken together at length about the pros and cons of our application. We do both understand the position which you set out. The main reason for our visa request is simply that we would like our son to visit distant cousins in America and so experience a new country early in his life. Our cousins ·have on many occasions asked us to visit them. Now seems such a good opportunity to travel while my husband is, as yet, not wholly recovered. Within a short time, we would hope to be able to return and then continue our life and work here as you have indicated."

The major seemed to be examining a particular spot on the ceiling. It was his turn again. He sighed before beginning.

"Frau Doktor, Frau Doktor. Please think. We have already so far, as you will have noticed, discounted any political implications of your husband's membership of this country's National Socialist Party and of his earlier, wilder, student predilections for the Communist creed. Putting politics for a moment to one side, have you and your husband also seriously appreciated the full financial implications of your move? You must surely realise that all your assets would remain here, your dental practice, your house and furniture, your bank and savings balances, jewellery, paintings, everything. You would also have to find resources to pay our administration to look after your properties, to maintain them in good order while you are away and, of course, we would in addition also expect your agreement for the withdrawal of regular monies from your estate to enable us to pay the salaries of your employees until such time as you return."

Another pause…

Back again to his mother. The boy waited, trying to look away from her.

Ilona now leant far forward. Only the large desk prevented closer contact. She smiled the gentlest of smiles. "Yes, Herr Major, thank you. Thank you for the breadth of your advice. I do so much appreciate your objectivity. Please do not think me ungrateful. On this particular occasion, if your understanding and kindness could be so far-reaching… then we would still welcome the opportunities which an exit visa would open for my son, my husband and for myself." She lingered on the word 'myself'. Jan had not before that moment been aware that his mother's eyes could glow.

As the major stood up, the boy knew that the last scene had arrived. The wrinkled head hovered towards mother and son, then back again over the papers on the desk. He sighed another, longer sigh, before moving slowly over to a window. To Jan's surprise, his mother also stood up. She seemed to be swaying slightly. At the window, the major turned towards them. Then he processed back, finally coming to a standstill under his leader. Tilting his head to one side, he began his formal statement.

"Frau Doktor Dusek, I have reached my decision. I have to tell you that I am, most reluctantly, persuaded." Then, with a rush: "Arrangements will be made for the preparation of your family passports and exit visas. These will be ready and available for collection from the main office downstairs in three days' time." With a further, even more abrupt, "*Gute Reise!*" he proffered his hand across the desk.

Ilona, still swaying, reached far over the desk to return the handshake. He nodded to her, then to Jan, then waved them towards the doors. It was over. She had done it.

Their escort was still waiting on the landing to take them downstairs and out into the street. Ilona now embraced her son. She had some difficulty letting go.

"Let's tell your father the news."

In the small room on the second floor that evening, the mosquitoes were in a particularly powerful attack mode, but Jan was too tired to do battle. He slid his head and arms under the sheet from where, hot and sweating, he drifted into sleep, lulled by the voices of his parents, who seemed prepared to talk through the night.

Next morning, Jan remembered to ask his mother if she knew whether Rachel and her family had been given visas to go to Israel.

"There is still some uncertainty," Ilona replied.

Within days following the granting of the exit visas, his father seemed to make a miraculous recovery. Each day, he rose early and would often have completed a morning walk before it was time to join breakfast in the Krchmenkos' kitchen. His boisterous nature and his conversation once again began to be laced with enriching comment. As of old, he would suddenly lunge forward to encircle his wife within the ring of his arms, again and again calling her his darling little Ilona. She would be torn between worry for his heart condition and delight to be once again so courted. At mealtimes, he would begin to introduce philosophical concepts into the everyday conversations, a habit not all the other lodgers appreciated. He even joined his wife at the consulate to collect the stamped passport and exit visas which had, with Teutonic thoroughness, been promptly made ready for the third day following Ilona's interview, all as promised.

The remainder of the first two weeks of August were spent in a flurry of activity, with Jan joining his mother and father during meetings and visits and at the saying of goodbyes. It seemed that there were a considerable number of occasions for weeping. Within the house, the lodgers were pleased for the Duseks, but by comparison became even more concerned for their own unresolved futures.

On the morning of 19th August, the last house farewells were held in the kitchen. Jan was much hugged. Afterwards, the family of three stood outside the front door waiting for a summoned taxi, the journey cost of which was to be their last item of expenditure in this land. They carried coats. On the pavement by their feet stood their one small suitcase, a honeymoon relic measuring forty by thirty by ten centimetres deep, now holding their entire worldly possessions. Next to the suitcase, Jan's small rucksack was filled with a picnic which the Krchmenkos had carefully prepared. Madame K and her daughter, each still wearing an apron though breakfast was over, were circling around the departing trio. At the sight of the approaching taxi, both women grew more agitated and tried simultaneously to embrace Jan, with resulting confusion, before all five hugged and kissed for the last time. As the vehicle drew away, Jan knelt on the rear seat to look back. The two women were locked together in the form of a single-aproned figure with a double head.

3

AT PRAGUE'S WILSONOVA station there was no one to see them off. The departure platform for Vlissingen was crowded but, unlike the scenes of confusion they had witnessed on their arrival from Karlovy Vary, there was now a controlling order of watchfulness and fear.

"Why so many Gestapo?" Jan asked. "All those black uniforms. And who are the others in brown?"

"People call them 'brownshirts'." Ivan spoke quietly. "'*Braunhemden*', they call themselves, '*sturmabteilung*', they are Hitler's 'storm-troops'. Nasty lot."

Ilona was anxious to move on. Ivan straightened up and took charge again, leading the family to a particular coach and compartment halfway along the waiting train. They settled into three of the eight allocated seats, of which the remaining five were soon also filled. Jan, the only child in the group, was given a place by the window. His father told him with a smile that he would be travelling backwards all the way through Germany to Holland in the west. Next to Jan, nearer the train corridor, were his mother and two older, grey-haired and silent women. In the window seat directly opposite Jan sat a thinly haired man in a light suit, who was staring out of the window. Like Jan, he seemed unable to keep still, constantly dabbing his forehead with a white handkerchief. Beside him sat Ivan, seemingly relaxed, already reading from a worn book: Schopenhauer's *The World as Will and Representation*. Between his father and the corridor screen, a white-haired couple murmured constantly to each other as they examined documents which they regularly lifted from, then replaced into, a handbag.

The compartment's door to the corridor was now closed. Two piercing whistles on the platform were followed by a belching of steam as the train pulled away. Ivan looked up to exchange a glance with his wife.

Another train journey. Jan enjoyed looking out of the window at the Czech countryside as towns and villages slid past. There was little movement along the corridor, while in the compartment all seemed engrossed with their own thoughts, unprepared to communicate. After about half an hour, the train stopped at a siding.

"Probably the border with Germany," his father said.

An SS officer opened the compartment door. "*Guten morgen. Papiere bitte.*" He was curt, polite, quick, glancing only in a perfunctory manner at the papers offered up to him. After a brief round, he gave them a '*danke*' with a saluted '*heil Hitler, gute reise*', before leaving.

In the corner opposite Jan, the man in the light suit turned to them all. "That was so surprising, so short. He even wished us a good trip. I can hardly believe it. I had expected difficulties. But then, I suppose we still have the border crossing between Germany and Holland." The others nodded. Soon, the train moved on.

In the following hours, their journey progressed steadily across Germany. Jan continued his watch at the window. There was now more activity in the corridor as passengers queued for toilets and uniformed men passed, carrying clipboards. These activities interested the boy, while the adults, with the exception of Jan's father, buried deep in his book, looked away.

By mid-afternoon, no further figure of authority had entered the compartment. Any remaining reserve between the eight travellers had evaporated. Sandwiches, fruit and drinks had been exchanged. All had begun to tell their stories. The two women next to Ilona were Jana and Gallina, sisters from Prague, about to join a brother who had worked for years in London in the import-export business. The couple on one side of Ivan, Herr and Frau Mares, were also travelling to London to join their son, a linguist and translator working with a publishing firm. The light-suited man opposite Jan had introduced himself as Herr Weiner. He did not speak of relatives. He said he was 'in films'.

The developing conversations included much anxiety. Herr Mares cautioned that they should all be careful; there could be Gestapo agents on the train.

Meanwhile, the sisters whispered to Ilona, seeking reassurance. "We have been told that women will be taken off the train at random when we reach the final border station… apparently SS females with dirty gloves feel around deep inside one to prevent smuggling jewellery, like rings… we understand that sometimes the train pulls out across the border while such a search, such molestation, is still going on, so the searched women never ever get back to their loved ones... do you think that this can be true?"

Ilona made reassuring sounds, though she could not answer the question.

Herr Weiner was also becoming agitated. "The Czech border was too easy, don't you think?" he asked Jan's father. "You can't trust them... please could you look over my papers... I've done everything correctly, haven't I? ...I've signed everything, left all my possessions behind as they wanted... here are copies of the documents, here is the copy letter from my guarantor in London, my dated exit visa, my passport, my train ticket, everything... surely there will be no problems at the final border?"

Ivan, like his wife, tried to be positive, saying that all the papers certainly seemed to be in order. Even then, Herr Weiner was unwilling to be placated.

"Please look more carefully... as a doctor you may see some items or clauses which may give rise to misunderstanding, to questioning... if you see even the smallest thing, please tell me... I may need to have extra answers ready."

Ivan again looked slowly at each item before repeating his earlier view. What else could he say to help this man?

Herr Weiner now addressed everyone: "When they come again, we must all appear to be at ease. I will personally be extremely business-like."

By early evening, the train was moving more slowly. Outside the compartment window, daylight was fading over the suburbs of a large city. It was the quiet Herr Mares who set the scene for the others.

"This could be Essen. The last checks could be made here before we travel further to the Dutch border, close by."

They could hear the train's brakes being applied, then a clattering of the carriages as the train came to a halt alongside a platform, on which only uniformed groups were waiting. At the dark back of the platform, a light inside an office window brightly framed some figures, leaning over what might have been paperwork.

Jan looked around at the grown-ups, who were all silent. His mother gave his hand a squeeze, which only increased the beating of his heart. The train corridor now became noisy. Doors were opened. Orders were issued. This place was busier than the Czech/German border.

Soon, louder voices reached the next compartment, and shortly afterwards, three men in the black uniform of the SS appeared at the doorway. Jan at once noticed their unusual peaked caps, on which were displayed skull-and-crossbones emblems, like those he had seen in his book on pirates which had been left behind in the villa. But this wasn't a book or a game. Two of the men stepped forward.

"*Reisepässe und visa vorzeigen, zugtickets bitte!*"

The sisters and Frau Mares, all three nearest the door, were the first to offer up their papers. Both sisters were trembling. Each SS man thumbed the offerings, staring intently at passport photographs and comparing these with the strained faces below. In each case, there followed a stamping procedure, a quick '*danke*', a click of shiny heels and the documents were handed back. Then it was the turn of Jan's father, who had to place Schopenhauer to one side so that he could hold up the full set of family papers. These also received only minimum attention before another '*danke*' and more heel clicking. Jan decided he would later experiment with that heel-clicking stuff, alongside the swivelling.

The first man now moved towards the window to stand in front of the seated Herr Weiner, who had pressed himself hard into his corner, trying to appear nonchalant by waving his papers in an offhand way towards the blackness before him. Perhaps such nonchalance produced the wrong reaction because this time the response was slower, more deliberate. The SS man raised each single document into the air, affecting close scrutiny, before also passing selected items backwards to his companion. At a moment when Herr Weiner's open passport was being handed across, Jan could read the letters '*Jude*' stamped heavily across a page. Herr Weiner's forehead was dripping with sweat as he searched helplessly in his pocket for the white handkerchief. He half rose from his corner, then fell back again.

"You will find everything in order. Everything has been agreed in the consulate in Prague. The permit has been signed by the Head of the Gestapo in the Protectorate… and in any case, your colleague at the Czech border has already seen and passed the documents."

The first man took a slow, deep breath, the kind of intake one might have before confronting a naughty child. He became particularly polite, looking round to his companion as if for moral support. "Yes, yes, of course, but there are other matters to be checked. There is the question of your age, for example, which does not appear to have been included in the papers. So, please, would you now come with us?"

This was not what Herr Weiner wanted to hear. He became aggressive, his body shaking, his voice higher-pitched. "No, I will not leave this train! You cannot do this! My documents are in order! They are properly stamped! My age has nothing to do with the matter!" He waved an arm around the compartment. "Where are the ages on my friends' documents?" His challenge hung in the air.

The third SS officer began to move forwards into the compartment. He waited. Everyone waited.

This time, Herr Weiner spoke quietly. "I have given you everything. Why do you need me also?"

There was no reply. Without further coercion, Herr Weiner slid forwards to his feet. He then tried an end gambit: "My suitcase, what about my suitcase? Shall I bring it with me or leave it here for my return?"

The first SS man shrugged his shoulders. "It doesn't matter to me." He stood to one side to clear a route to the door. Herr Weiner stumbled forward, leaving his suitcase on the rack. The suitcase might yet be his insurance policy. Out in the corridor he paused, looked back once and bowed formally in the direction of Jan's father. At later times in his life, Jan would often remember Herr W's gentle, calm, resigned, yet at the same time theatrical, bow, before he disappeared along the corridor, closely escorted by the three men of the SS.

Stillness hung over the compartment. Jana and Gallina held each other's shaking hands. Jan whispered to his mother, "Why Herr Weiner? Why did they want to know his age?"

Ilona shook her head several times.

Not long afterwards, the train moved slowly out of the station and into the night. Uniformed Germans could no longer be seen. Were they still on board? Herr Weiner's corner seat remained unoccupied. The suitcase on the rack was left untouched.

Jan kept thinking, *He has left his suitcase… he has left his suitcase*. Unable to concentrate further, he laid his head on his mother's lap and fell asleep.

Just before dawn, the train again stopped. Herr Mares said, "If this is the real border, we have been told that a Dutch conductor will replace the German conductor. There will apparently be no further checks." Minutes later the journey recommenced, while along the full length of the corridor there were sounds of cheering.

On the morning of 20th August 1939, the train arrived on the harbourside at Vlissingen. As the sleepy and befuddled passengers carried their few belongings down the carriage steps, they half expected again to be herded, categorised and shouted at. Instead, there were only the sounds of port activity, of shouts which accompanied the loading and off-loading of foods on cargo ships at several quaysides.

No one interrupted the newcomers. They could look around, stretch, talk to anyone, make their own decisions. They could see that an existing crowd, which had arrived on an earlier train, was starting to move towards a large passenger boat anchored at a nearby quay. The new arrivals joined the flow. Then there were some necessary official directions, but given with kindness and concern. Through the morning the boat's decks and salons slowly filled with migrants, all for the most part trance-like but happy.

At noon, the loaded vessel moved out of the harbour. Within an hour, a warm sun reinforced the general growing sense of security. Ivan and Ilona, who had stayed awake during the night's train journey, stretched out to sleep on the wooden top deck. Jan was their guardian of a kind, climbing railings nearby, scanning the horizon. He had never been to sea before. This was so new, so wonderful. Around his sleeping father and mother, the crowded passengers formed endless patterns of free activity, talking, arguing, laughing, even sunbathing. Jan was starting to play a game of balance on the top-but-one railing when a nearby shout caused him to lose his footing. Quickly upright again, he became aware of people pointing ahead. He could see that what had been a hazy edge between water and sky was now a long, thin, white line, on which more and more people were concentrating. He woke his parents. All three leaned with others against the railings. His father lifted him onto the very top rail and supported him there.

"Look, my son, look. That white line is chalk, just like the chalk used on your kindergarten blackboard. It is a long line of cliffs called the White Cliffs of Dover. You are looking at England. Ahead of us is England!"

Now, all those who could walk or stand were on deck, straining to look ahead. Children were lifted onto shoulders. The level of noise, which had increased dramatically at the sighting of the shoreline, now suddenly dropped. All that could be heard was the wind and the splash of the boat's bow cutting through the waves. Then, someone somewhere on deck began to cry. Then more people wept. Then others began to weep and laugh simultaneously. Among the commotion, some fell to their knees and began to pray. Others followed. In the afternoon sunshine, the boat was filled with laughing and weeping and praying people.

His father lifted Jan back onto the deck before pulling a shining object out of an inside jacket pocket. It was a thin silver cigarette case. When he was older, Jan reflected on how his father could so openly have brought a silver item across two guarded borders, or why a doctor with a heart condition should have been smoking at all. Ivan drew himself to his full height. Brandishing the precious possession high in the air he practised two circular swinging movements before giving a joyful shout as he threw the cigarette case far out into the waters of the English Channel. Turning to his wife, he declared he was giving up smoking, a promise which he kept. Whether he would smoke again or not, Ilona could not understand why her husband had discarded an object of such value now that they were poor.

"Why are you so impractical? It is all that philosophy." They embraced each other.

4

THE SHIP'S ARRIVAL at a new harbour spread general renewed anxiety among the tired travellers. Families and friends searched for each other along the quayside. Possessions were closely guarded as immigration staff cajoled bewildered groups into queues lined in front of waiting coaches. Transport destinations were being loudly called out, unknown place names which Jan had never before heard but which sounded interesting. He did recognise the call 'London' as his father said, "Come on, that's for us." The trio, with their small suitcase, climbed aboard for whatever lay ahead. As the coach gathered momentum and lights flashed in the darkness outside the window, Jan, wedged between his parents, soon fell asleep.

The two remaining weeks of August in this new land appeared to the boy to be like a kaleidoscope with fast-changing variations. Even the warm weather was unsettled, turning from rain to thunderstorms and lightning. Jan missed the company of other children. He seemed often to be looking upwards to grown-ups, who were looking down on him. Constant change included walking with his parents along different streets framed by different houses, before standing in different doorways where his parents would then speak to different people in a language he did not understand. Sometimes these conversations would lead to a night or nights in an unfamiliar room, before another morning meant moving on again.

Then suddenly, in the last days of the month, the Duseks settled down.

"It's just one room," his mother said. "But look, we have an open fireplace where we can burn wood to keep ourselves warm in the winter. And look outside the window; there's that nice street of houses and a hillside which leads up to a beautiful park. And the lady of the house, Mrs Brown, says that we can cook in her kitchen. Aren't we lucky?"

The trio agreed on their luck. In those new days of safety, Jan could sense a yet further increase of his parents' energies. Suddenly, both went out on 'errands', as they had done in Prague, his mother returning with provisions for them all, including drawing materials for himself and writing materials for herself and Ivan. His father would bring back a newspaper which he would at once study intensely. Often within only hours of such an 'errand', his mother would cheerfully ask Jan to accompany her on a walk out again to post letters 'in a special red posting box'.

On the first of September, a Friday, Ivan was away for many hours. He returned in the late afternoon, clutching a newspaper.

"Look at this *London Evening Standard*… the headlines

don't need much translation, even for a six-year-old like you, Jan.

> "'GERMANS INVADE & BOMB POLAND.
> BRITAIN MOBILISES.
> Ten Polish Towns Bombed. Danzig Annexed'.

"Their troops crossed the Polish frontier at dawn this morning. They will do to the rest of Europe what they did to us Czechs. So, what now? Great Britain and France have promised to defend Poland. There will be war."

On 2nd September, Ivan again returned from an outing with a further *Evening Standard*. This time, Ilona read and translated for their son:

> "'GERMANS RESUME ATTACK AS MPs MEET'."

Ivan was able to add: "At any moment now, there could be a war. The papers also remind us that 'blackout' regulations came into force last night: all lights inside the windows and doors of buildings must from sunrise to sunset be 'obscured', as they say, with curtains or cardboard. We must ask the Browns what they want us to use and if they have some old materials."

On the morning of Sunday 3rd September, Mr Brown knocked on the Duseks' door. "The Prime Minister is going to broadcast to the nation at eleven o'clock. Would you like to listen with Mrs Brown and me in the kitchen?"

The Duseks agreed to be there. More news in a kitchen, just like Prague all over again.

By 11.00am, all five were waiting together. Jan was restless. Mr Brown tried talking to him: "Our Prime Minister is called Mr Neville Chamberlain."

Jan nodded. At the precise moment of 11.15am, the kitchen became filled by a reedy voice, which continued steadily for a few minutes. Jan saw how still the others were as they listened. Only once during the broadcast did his father nod vigorously. Later, Ivan translated for the boy.

"'*He can only be stopped by force.*' Those were the words which Chamberlain used. So right, at last. His words were simple… '*This country is at war with Germany.*'"

Back in their room that afternoon, Ivan called for a family conference.

"Let us make plans. This will be a long war. It could cover the world. Already France, Australia, New Zealand and India have followed England to declare war on that man. Canada says it will follow. Then there will be others. We will not travel to America. We will become English; we will become what is called 'naturalised'. You, Jan, can start school in mid-September and will learn fast. Here at home, we will stop speaking Czech or bits of German and we will speak English only; won't that be exciting? Meanwhile, your mother and I will find work so that we can live. We are allowed to work because, as Czechs, we are called 'friendly aliens'."

By mid-September, Ivan's predictions were becoming real. "The news confirms that Russian troops have invaded Poland. The Poles had bitten into our Czech lands and now the Russians bite into Poland! What's wrong with us Eastern Europeans?"

September and October became months of acclimatisation for the trio. Jan began full-time school and would come home with news of friendships forged, with little need for language. He would laughingly recite newly acquired playground doggerel with dubious meanings… all happily accepted by his parents as learning advancement. On one evening, they laughed when Jan told them the story of that day's main school event. A woman teacher had asked him a question he did not understand.

"Do you speak Italian?"

"Yes."

He had then been escorted down a long corridor and into a new classroom.

"It was full of big girls."

"What happened?" his father asked.

"I cried."

On their side, Ivan and Ilona also made new contacts, applied for advertised jobs, sent away applications for naturalisation. Progress was slow. One day, an official-looking letter arrived, addressed to Doctors Ivan and Ilona Dusek, bringing news which was relayed by Ilona to Jan that evening.

"Our president Beneš and our Czech 'government-in-exile' are here in England. They are going to give us some money to live on until we can find work. Two pounds and fifty pence English money for all of our family food and lodging per week. We should be able to manage that, even to include your father's daily newspaper and even something for your own first English pocket money, hurrah!"

From then onwards, Ivan was able to search the *Evening Standard* each day and would relay further essential war information, together with his own personal reflections, to his wife, whether Ilona was in receptive mood or not, and to his young son, whether Jan fully understood or not. Ivan also found common ground with Mr Brown, who was retired, as both men discussed the day's events in the Browns' kitchen over mugs of tea. Mrs Brown took no part in these talks. Although accepting the immigrants' rent, she continued to be uncertain about her lodgers. Sometimes in the evening, when Ivan, Ilona and Jan were talking, they could hear the creaking of floorboards just outside their room door. Jan would point to the door.

"Never mind," his father would whisper. "It's quite funny, really. Mrs Brown is listening because she thinks we may be spies."

The Duseks' fireplace was put to use, with lighting wood and coal bought at low cost from the Browns. Weekends became family times, with no school for Jan, no job seeking for his parents. All three, together with newfound friends from Jan's school – children and parents, English and immigrant – would make outings to that large park called Richmond, where all were thrilled by the slow-moving herds of deer and the great-antlered stags.

The same friends joined in two end-of-year celebrations. At the end of November, Jan had a seventh birthday party, followed closely by the Duseks' first English Christmas. Mrs Brown had by now relented. She and Ilona had become close friends in the kitchen, where they exchanged details of national cooking habits. Ilona accepted Mrs Brown's 'I am Doris' advice with pleasure, though she held firm by cooking fish on Christmas Eve and persuading Ivan and Jan to join in her walk to the nearest church service for midnight mass.

The New Year of 1940 became colder. One morning in mid-January, when Jan looked out of the window he started jumping for joy. "Snow! Snow! Look, look, it's just like home! Just the same as home. When can we go out?"

Going and coming from school was such pleasure; there were snowball fights and sliding competitions and building snow fortifications. But his greatest pleasure was reserved for the weekend because Ivan had told him: "You and I will have a mission…"

On Saturday morning, with snow flurries still falling, father and son borrowed sacks from Mr Brown and made their way up to the boundaries of Richmond Park. Here, the pair slowly worked their way along the hedgerows, Ivan as chief, Jan as second-in-command, both systematically raiding the snow-covered foliage, picking up, breaking and binding hundreds of fallen twigs, which they then stored tightly in the sacks. After only a rest at lunchtime for salami, bread and water, the pair's movements through the day became ever more regular, coordinated, untroubled by others, just boy and father alone in the vast, winter emptiness of the park, watched only by the soft eyes of the passing herds of deer.

That evening, the fireplace in the Duseks' room glowed and crackled. Jan was tired with pleasure. There were no longer creaking sounds outside the door.

The late English winter changed imperceptibly into early spring. Jan, too, was changing fast. His growing body revelled in playground football. His English vocabulary increased daily, allowing room for both Cockney slang and a sufficient spread of the 'King's English' so that he could share daily newspaper articles with his father.

"See how this helps him learn not only about language but also about the world," Ivan would tell his wife.

"You don't need to push him quite so much," Ilona would respond. "Fortunately, he best likes those cartoons by David Low!"

The early 1940 months provided a lull for the Duseks. Ivan, as if on guard with the *Standard*, knew too well that, as he put it, "All hell will soon break loose." His soothsaying was proved correct, much to his sadness. From April onwards, he relayed the daily news of German armies sweeping into France and of their battles against the combined French and English retreating forces. On 10th May, it was Mr Brown who broke fresh news.

"Just through on the wireless... Chamberlain has resigned! Churchill is Prime Minister!"

Four days later, all channels of publication told of German troops invading the Low Countries. At the end of May, news of tragedy and heroism reached Jan's school and home simultaneously, news around a name which he would add to his vocabulary. That name was 'Dunkirk'. Ivan explained what was happening:

"The Germans have forced a whole English army back to the sea which separates France from England. Hundreds of English ships of all sizes have sailed out to bring the soldiers home. They are succeeding."

In late June, his mother broke fresh news of change. "Jan, we are going to move. I know that your summer term at school has not yet finished. Your father and I are sorry about that, especially since you have made such good friends. But we will only be moving from here in Richmond to a nearby place called Hounslow, so we think you will still be able to stay in touch with some of those friends. I have been able to find work in Hounslow. I am going to make hats, which is called being a 'milliner'. This will help us all because we will have a little more money and so will be able to live in more space than this one room. And there will be lots of new things for you to discover, a new part of London, a new school, new friends, new adventures." Jan's head filled with questions while his mother had been talking, but the words 'new adventures' pulled him round, as Ilona knew they would.

Goodbyes were said to his friends at school and to his teachers. There were handshakes with Mr Brown and hugs with Mrs Brown, both now friends of the family.

One early evening, days later, Jan found himself standing with his parents and their single suitcase alongside a busy street roundabout. Cars were splashing rain over the pavement. "Here we are then!" his father announced cheerfully. In front of them grey steps led to the grey front door of a grey building. "Many people live here," his father said. "We will be sharing the ground-floor apartment with a married couple who are due to arrive tomorrow."

Once inside, Ivan led the way along a dark corridor to a further door, which opened onto several rooms, all in darkness.

"We'll have light soon, very special light," he said. "Gas lamps. Let's be explorers!"

His father found long sticks. "They are called tapers," Ivan said, before lighting the sticks with matches and then offering them up to holes in the ceiling lamps, each of which jumped into a warm light and made gentle fizzing noises. The rooms were explored and claims on space established. Supper followed: delicious red cabbage with apple, cooked in their own kitchen. Then long talking, this time not always in English, then deep sleep, with Jan once again in a room of his own.

Next day, the front doorbell, on which Jan had been experimenting with various pushing techniques, rang without his efforts. Two people introduced themselves. They were Maurice and Betty Tope, who were to occupy two of the four bedrooms, while sharing the flat's bathroom, kitchen and living room. That evening in the living room, the Duseks and the Topes soon became acquainted. Betty was a shy person who seemed to have few personal opinions but instead agreed with everything her husband had to say. Maurice, on the other hand, was full of voice and self-assurance.

"That man Hitler can't really be as bad as people make out. Didn't he rightly lift his people out of the subjugation which we had all forced on his nation after the Great War? If we had only befriended him then, this present war would never have started. I'm certainly not going to fight in it. I've registered as a conscientious objector, whatever people may think of me."

Ilona looked over to her husband, but Ivan was looking at his shoes. Then he said, "Why don't we all have an early night on this, our first evening together?"

In subsequent weeks, Ivan spoke little to Maurice. "It's best if we stay calm," he told Ilona. "After all, we are visitors here."

The Duseks soon re-established their daily lives. Ilona left the new home early each morning for work as a milliner in a hat shop on Hounslow High Street. Her husband would tease her: "Is that why you studied medicine in Vienna? Is that why you went to Freud's lectures? To design and make pretty hats?" For his part, Ivan continued to send off job application forms and letters. Even when there were no replies or when applications were rejected, he remained positive and continued searching.

Jan had been excited to hear that his new school was only two streets away and would be open until mid-July, the start of summer holidays. "When can I go?" he asked. "Now I can walk to school by myself!" A week later, he was already sitting at a classroom desk, among new faces, listening to a new teacher. In the playground, his classmates crowded round, wanting to know about him, where he had come from, where he lived. It did not matter that he answered briefly; of more importance was that he could play football, so he was OK.

At the end of the school week, there was a knock at the Duseks' door. A new classmate of Jan's introduced himself.

"I'm Terry Busby. Can Jan come out to play football?" Ilona and Ivan looked at each other.

"Where do you play?"

"Round the back." Terry said. "We always play on a Saturday."

Only for a brief further moment did Ilona and Ivan hesitate.

"Of course," they said. It was time to let go.

Terry had a gang, the Bees, in which Jan became the new recruit. For the rest of the summer and autumn months of 1940, he took part in all the gang's activities. Football was played in a yard among industrial buildings behind the Duseks' lodgings. Ilona would sigh when she washed Jan's shirts, which had acted as goalposts, or when scuffed shoes needed repair. Ivan would be brought in to talk to the boy when he returned from a gang foray with bleeding knees or elbows.

"What were you all doing?"

"Nothing much… just climbing on walls and railings…"

Sometimes, other of the gang members' parents would join Ilona and Ivan to apologise to neighbours for their children's wilder ways. Only rarely would a border be crossed, such as when the gang returned from Hounslow's Saturday open market with satisfied, fruit-stained faces.

"What have you been eating?"

"Strawberries and things."

"Did you pay for them? You haven't? You must never take anything for which you haven't paid! Here's some money… go back and pay and say sorry."

From July to October, the gang's activities were overshadowed by conflict above their heads. Londoners who looked upwards could see war battles being fought in the skies. Planes circled planes in vicious manoeuvres to the death, manoeuvres which often ended when one combatant burst into flames, before screeching downwards in a ball of fire to explode over some random city location. Ivan would explain to his son: "The German Luftwaffe is fighting the English Royal Air Force. So much depends on this fight which they call 'The Battle of Britain'. We have to win, or Hitler will invade."

Sometimes, the Bees gang's street escapades were taking place even while the killing continued overhead. In such moments, Ilona and Ivan did not ask their son to come home.

"Let him play; if an aircraft is shot down it can crash anywhere," Ivan would rationalise.

By the end of August, two months into the air battles, Ilona's earnings had enabled Ivan to buy a wireless set. He could now follow the war via broadcasts as well as print. He would be optimistic: "I'm sure the English pilots are winning…"

Then, on a late afternoon in early September, just after Jan had come home from school, a long and loud sound, its pitch rising and falling alternately, filled the Hounslow streets. Ivan switched on the wireless.

"It's a warning signal. It seems that there will be bombing. The German air force is trying something new. The sound we hear is being made by air-raid sirens. We must stay together and wait."

That night in the living room, all five flat dwellers heard the endless droning of planes, the initial distant thumping of explosives, the defending gunfire and the wailing of ambulances. Just before midnight, there came a moment when a sudden, violent overhead explosion rocked the building. Maurice Tope threw himself across the room and under the heavy, old wooden dining table. Betty Tope and the Duseks watched him lying there, not re-emerging until a later single note siren announced the 'all-clear'.

"They have gone," said Ivan. "For the time being, we are spared."

Next day, Ivan relayed radio bulletin news: "The announcer spoke of London's East End, where the dockyards have been devastated by high explosives and incendiary bombs, with nearly two thousand people killed or harmed in the last single night. Apparently, German radio says that such bombing is set to continue over London and other English cities until victory is won. Hitler calls this his 'Blitzkrieg', his 'lightning war'. We now have Blitz and Battle of Britain combined."

During September and October weekends, Ivan and Ilona did not hold their son back from playing street games with his Bees gang friends. Jan would return from such excursions with descriptions of rubble being cleared where houses had once stood.

"On the other side of the warehouses, there are piles of bricks and wood and furniture... even toys which are still smoking."

All the gang's parents could only caution their children. "After all," Ivan would tell Ilona, "if we kept the boy at home, an invading bomb could just as easily drop on us here."

Night after night in the following weeks, the bombing continued under cover of the dark. Jan became familiar with the rise and fall of the sirens' opening warning tones, as well as the calming 'all-clear' message when a raid was over. Each evening, the Duseks, with hundreds of fellow Londoners, took themselves, with their coats and blankets, to the nearest underground railway station. There, on a crowded platform deep in the earth, children would still play before being called to join families stretched out to sleep safely till morning.

Each daylight brought the latest batch of statistics, of streets no longer existing, of the dead and injured numbers.

When Jan listened to the radio with his father, he learnt the names of English cities: Plymouth, Southampton, Bristol, Birmingham, Coventry.

"They are also being bombed," Ivan said.

At the end of October, the national news bulletins declared that the Battle of Britain was won, that the Luftwaffe's marauding fighter raids had ended. At supper, Ivan called for a toast with water glasses. "To the Royal Air Force!" he declared. "To those brave pilots!" Then, he cautioned: "But the Blitz and the bombers are still coming. They will lose; they will also lose…"

Life went on in spite of the daily destruction. Change was evident everywhere. Food rationing was established. On each Saturday morning, Jan stood with his mother and the family ration book, waiting patiently in shopping queues for weekly provisions.

"Better than the Prague consulate queue, remember?" she asked him. "And only a little red meat, so much better for your father's angina."

The bombing continued through November, past Jan's eighth birthday and into December. Jan and his friends, on their way to school each morning, would check to see if any of the giant silver 'barrage' balloons, newly suspended in the skies, had entangled any of the enemy's planes, but there was no such evidence.

Each day, Ilona continued to go to work. "For whom do you make hats at this time?" Ivan asked. "Who buys now?" Ivan's own applications for employment were making little progress. Then, one week before Christmas, his optimism was answered. A large envelope arrived addressed to Doctor

Dusek and bearing on one corner the sign of a feathered animal, whose long neck was encircled by a gold crown.

"Look, a *cestina*, just like those on the Tepla." Jan was excited.

"Here, it is called 'swan'," his mother said. "Please, give the letter to your father."

When all three were gathered, Ivan opened the envelope formally. A brief glance at the contents brought out his broadest of smiles. "They have accepted my papers. I have been given work. I am to be the Chief School Dental Officer for the English county of Buckinghamshire…"

Ilona was smiling at her husband, her hand on his shoulder, even as Jan was hurling out questions: "Where is Buckinghamshire? Is it near? Will it be near enough for me to go on seeing my school friends?"

His parents' replies talked of new friends, new adventures, of still more change. They had their own questions, many yet without answers. Their optimism outweighed any misgivings.

Throughout the days of Christmas 1940 and the early new year of 1941, Jan's parents tried to make practical plans, their discussions often continuing in the underground railway station as the nightly bombing of London continued. Whenever possible, Jan played with the Bees gang, storing up memories. Sometimes the footballers, in chase of a ball, would turn a corner into what had once been a street. No longer. Instead, the darkness of house terrace fronts alternated with the lightness of sky above empty gaps, at the feet of which the remnants of lives had been hurriedly shovelled.

5

IN MID-JANUARY 1941 the Duseks moved on. They found themselves in their latest home in the rural community of Buckingham. Ivan's salary allowed them to rent four high-ceilinged rooms on the ground floor of a four-storeyed house. Similar large, detached houses lined one side of their street, which was in a valley. On the other side of the street grew tall trees, edging a hillside. During the first weeks of the family's arrival, the trees, the hillside, the streets and the houses were all covered in layers of snow, which the skies replenished daily.

On the day after their arrival, Ivan announced, "Let us march out and explore. I've been studying the map… Buckingham is a small county town which will feel so different to Hounslow, to London."

Jan was already ahead of his parents, making every move twice in the whiteness, crunching the snow under his feet. On one side of their front door, the street curved and ended at a small railway station. The other direction led them into town. Ivan strode on as guide. First, they passed a small corner building marked 'Chandos'.

"Aha! We are living near the town cinema, how interesting. Jan, you will be able to see your first English film."

They crossed a bridge over a narrow river 'like the Tepla but smaller', then upwards into a wide market square.

"Look how the square slopes steeply, like Wenceslas Square. Apparently, there is a market here twice a week, and the school dental clinic where I will work is also located here. Look, beyond the square is another open space filled with railed enclosures, perhaps pens for cattle and other animals." But by then Jan had found a small stone building with turrets which reminded him of a corner piece of Prague Castle.

As the early months of 1941 merged into spring, so the three Czechs merged into their new life. They shared the house with four others whom they befriended. The first, Mr Francis, worked on a local farm instead of doing military service.

"He is called a conscientious objector, like Mr Tope in London," Ilona explained to Jan. "He does not believe in killing people."

The others were the Mansfields, a mother and her two daughters, younger than Jan. Mr Mansfield was away in the army 'serving with the Royal Engineers in the Far East', Mrs Mansfield said. All seven usually met when the air-raid sirens sounded. There was the option of going out to the back garden where their home's half-underground shelter, poorly constructed with timbers and corrugated metal sheeting, was stored with tinned provisions and damp blankets. Alternatively, there was the empty lower ground floor of the house, a cellar protected by the floors above. To this space, the house dwellers would usually retreat. The cellar 'would do' because, here in north Buckinghamshire, the sirens only warned of the occasional bombs dropped by enemy planes as they were returning from big raids in the Midlands and now needed to lighten their loads before attempting to return to Germany. Some of the seven, distributed around the floor, would try to sleep. Ivan would read.

Ivan's first earnings allowed Jan to become the owner of a second-hand bicycle, which he used on his explorations around the town. But going to his latest new school meant walking. He could walk from the house to school in ten minutes on a route which took him alongside the Chandos cinema, over the town bridge, then on a sharp left turn into the small school courtyard sheltered by a huddle of red-roofed houses and the Methodist Church. At school, he made friends quickly. The children in this small community bonded easily with each other. He was not the only new pupil in the spring term. Several boys and girls had also arrived from London as 'evacuees'. On the first day of term, the class teacher asked them to tell the other children about the 'Blitz'.

Jan relayed to Ivan and Ilona: "While their parents stay in the 'Blitz', my friends are now living with Buckingham families until the bombing is over. They listen to the radio each day, just as we do. After the London children, it was my turn to tell the class about our homeland and what had happened to us."

Soon after the start of the term, his father asked, "What are you learning about English history?" To Jan's vague reply,

Ivan said, "Right then, we are going to the pictures! The Chandos cinema is showing a film called *Lady Hamilton*. It's about a famous English admiral, Horatio Nelson. You'll learn some history and, anyway, your mother will love it. She will probably need her handkerchief."

That Saturday afternoon, Jan saw a film for the second time in his life. The cinema was warm. The purple seats were crowded. The story of love and battle, of triumph and disaster, engulfed the viewers. Laurence Olivier as Lord Nelson was handsome and heroic, a true Englishman and leader who would inevitably conquer his country's enemies. Vivien Leigh as Lady Hamilton was beautiful and intelligent, a true Englishwoman who would follow her heart wherever it led. The audience was captivated, Jan among them. The celluloid black and white struggles, the seas, sails and guns of the battle of Trafalgar would always remain lodged in his head, alongside the real battles of his childhood.

Ivan began his new career with enthusiasm. Early each morning, he too left the house to walk over to the market square where the school dental surgery, with its two well-equipped rooms, looked out over the centre of town. Here, Ivan, together with his dental nurse Joan, welcomed children who arrived from nearby schools throughout the day to have examinations or treatments. Ivan had always been a good dentist. Had he not successfully treated the cream of the international visitors during Karlovy Vary's summer season? Now, in this new setting, his jovial nature and caring attitude soon melted worries. Parents and teachers in Buckingham and in the surrounding villages grew to know and like the sturdy Czech who had arrived among them. But there was a snag.

Dental inspections also had to be carried out in the schools throughout the wider north Bucks area. Ivan could not drive.

One Friday in mid-March, Ivan returned later than usual from work.

"Come outside, you two, surprise, surprise…" he said.

Jan was first to leap to the front door. At the roadside stood a small car, black on top and rear, red on both door sides, with two round, protruding headlights and with side steps suspended between curved front and rear wheel guards. Jan gaped and Ilona said, "What have you done?"

"It's called a Morris Eight, second-hand, of course. I've been taking lessons in lunch hours and today passed a driving test. The examiner was probably too kind…"

All three walked around the car several times, Jan jumping in and out and stroking the headlights. "When can we have a ride?"

Ivan promised a trip to the countryside.

From that weekend onwards, the visits of Dr Dusek and his Morris Eight, properly loaded with dental equipment, became familiar sights at schools around north Buckinghamshire. Ivan would return home full of happiness. "The teachers and children are all so welcoming," he would say, before lifting Ilona into the air and exclaiming, "My little Ilerlie," and swinging her round in a full circle as he had done long ago.

Ilona, too, had her agendas. While her son and husband left for school and clinic each day, she was making friends with other school parents and connecting herself to the town's social groups. She became a member of the Buckingham Women's Guild, where her sewing skills were put to use in extra garment-making for the troops. As a Protestant, she joined the local Methodist Church and persuaded Ivan and Jan to go with her to Sunday services.

"We are all linked," she told Jan. "The teaching of our own Czech preacher, Jan Hus, will have influenced the Methodists' Charles Wesley."

Whether Jan understood his mother or not, he certainly enjoyed singing some of Wesley's hymns at Sunday evensong. Equally enjoyable were the afternoon teas at the Reverend and Mrs Jones's house a few doors away on Chandos Road, in the direction of the railway station. The minister's wife made marvellous cakes.

The Buckingham days of 1941 stayed tranquil for the Duseks while war raged further away.

"We have so many friends now." Ilona seemed almost surprised. "And in so short a time. The English are so kind. We are so fortunate."

In May, the German blitzkrieg bombing suddenly came to an end. "They've stopped choosing destruction here," Ivan said. "Because they need their planes to attack Russia. But the damage here in England is so bad... published numbers tell of over thirty thousand killed and nearly ninety thousand wounded and with sixty per cent of the casualties just in London. They estimate that one third of London has been destroyed."

Jan said that the parents of his evacuee friends were well and still sending letters.

On a day just before the summer holidays, Jan came home from school to find a khaki-uniformed soldier drinking coffee in the kitchen with Ilona. "Look who's here, dearest, your uncle František is here in England! What a surprise your father will have!"

"*Ahoj, jak se máš!*" František hugged the boy and started asking questions in Czech, to which Jan replied in English. Later, when Ivan returned from work, all four ate, drank and talked into the evening. His uncle said that he was able to stay overnight. "Tomorrow, I will rejoin my group. We are the Czech eleventh infantry battalion, serving under British commanders in the Allied North African Campaign, which has been going on for at least a year. After this leave, we know that we will shortly be posted out again. It is said that General Montgomery will lead our Eighth Army to engage with Rommel and his Axis forces before we try to invade Sicily. Who knows what will happen. I'm a world away from being a civil servant in Prague, from being a Wenceslas Square chess player."

Early next morning, his uncle gave Jan two packages wrapped with newspaper. "This heavier one I found for you in London, in the Charing Cross Road."

Jan opened the well-worn pages of *A Text Book on Practical Chess, the Praxis of My System* by Aaron Niemzowitsch. He sensed that he had been given a treasure.

"When you are older, we will play together," František said. "And we will perhaps play on this other present." He helped Jan to unravel a small, wooden chessboard, hinged at the centre to unload its contents of simply carved light and dark chess pieces. "I will show you how to set up a game. Your father can practise with you in preparation for our meeting. Look, you could start by placing the two beautiful and powerful queens, the dark queen on her dark square, the light queen on her light square. Remember, each queen likes her own colour: '*Regina amat suam colorem.*'"

It was time to go. The two brothers embraced. František asked, "Will you return, if ever possible?"

Ivan shook his head. "The boy is English now. We will make our lives here. What about you?"

Franto said he hoped one day to rejoin a new, free, Czech government 'after we have won this war'. Then, kitbag slung over his shoulder, he walked up the street towards the station. Jan waved until his uncle disappeared from sight.

All county-wide schools were closed for summer holidays. The Morris Eight rested. Ivan's dental treatment appointments continued only locally, in the Buckingham clinic, so that he was able to walk home each day to join his wife and son for a light lunch. Ilona liked preparing special salads, mixtures of vegetables and fruit, all dark and bright colours, aimed at protecting her man's heart condition. This meal pattern continued through a July of heat and thunderstorms, then into a cool August of rain. On a typical mid-August day of strong wind and rain, Ivan arrived for lunch as usual, but he was wet and shivering and, without changing into dry clothes, called for 'that lovely salad with that vinegar dressing', into which he tucked with relish. After only a few moments, he let out a growling, spluttering, coughing sound which he attempted to stifle as he slid to the floor.

Ilona threw back her chair and hurried to her husband. She bent over him, rubbing Ivan's chest and simultaneously telling Jan to please hurry and to please get on his bicycle and fetch the doctor from the surgery in the Market Square.

"Fast please, dearest. Tell him we have no telephone here."

The eight-year-old fought hard. He had not ridden his bike so fast before, had never bent his head so low, never clutched his handlebars so tightly. Now the wind and rain clouded his eyes, bound his shirt to his chest and beat at the legs which pounded the cycle pedals. In just minutes, the market square cobblestones reminded him of arrival. In the warm surgery, an elderly doctor, a war locum, understood the situation and drove at once with Jan back to the house.

From the room doorway, Jan watched the doctor join Ilona, her shoulders shaking, still bending over her husband on the floor. Ilona and the doctor spoke briefly together before turning to the boy. He could see that his mother's face was trickling with tears while she was also trying to bring up a smile. She reached to put an arm around his shoulder and drew him towards her.

"Jan, your father has died," she said.

Later, he could not remember whether he had cried as much as his mother had cried. He did recall them both trying to support each other. In the days which followed his father's death, a sequence of practical necessities suppressed the further flow of emotion. Much had to be done: letters had to be written, papers had to be completed, the funeral had to be arranged.

His father was buried in the Methodist section of Buckingham's cemetery, just outside the gates of Stowe School. A few friends stood by Ivan's grave as the Reverend Jones gave a short address. A cypress tree was planted to mark the burial place because a headstone could not yet be afforded.

In the following days of summer, Ilona had to consider the pair's financial situation. She explained to Jan, "We no longer have your father's salary, which took the place of the helpful allowance we had been given by the Czech government here in exile. Now, I must find work. Your father was able to show that he was a doctor and dentist because he had brought certificates with him to England, but I brought nothing. We will also need to move again; unfortunately, these nice rooms are now too expensive."

Jan's school autumn term began again in September, which became a month of further change.

"New news," Ilona said. "All so fast. I have been given a job. I am to be a school dental nurse in the system which employed your father. But the work is in the county town of Aylesbury, where we must find a home. And something even more exciting... the Czech government committee has written to say that they will pay for you to go to an English public school. That's a funny expression because here, public schools are really private schools, where parents pay for their children's education."

Jan was less enthusiastic. "Where will the school be? What about my friends here?"

"I'm sorry, dear; you will make many friends in your life, these next years will be so interesting; you will experience so much..." Shortly afterwards, Ilona added more detail. "The arms of the church are wide," she said. "The Reverend and Mrs Jones want you to stay with them while I start work in Aylesbury. Your new school is in another town to which you can travel each day on the local railway line."

Within a week, Ilona, carrying her small labelled

suitcase, was on board the bus to Aylesbury while Jan, with his rucksack and bicycle, became a member of the Jones household.

Public schools – in other words, 'private', Jan would remind himself – started only in late September, giving him time to settle into his latest new home. He now became one of four. The Reverend Jones was often away, attending meetings, visiting parishioners, holding services in his own or associated Methodist churches. Mrs Jones, large and kindly, ruled her vicarage home, comfortably organising gatherings whether under her own roof or in the church hall. The third 'grown-up' to whom Jan was formally introduced was a Miss Shuttleworth, 'a friend', Mrs Jones had said. Miss Shuttleworth was white-haired and walked painfully with a stick. Jan could understand why she sat reading for long hours in the living room's deepest armchair.

"Do you like reading?" she asked him, peering forwards through the strong lenses of her glasses.

He nodded.

"Then we must do some reading together. Do you like reading the bible?"

"I'm not sure."

"Then we must try together, perhaps in the evenings when you come back from school, or sometimes on a Sunday."

He decided not to reply. Perhaps this was what his mother meant about the arms of the church being wide.

6

JAN'S FIFTH NEW English school – 'public school', he reminded himself – began just before his ninth birthday. On an early autumnal morning, the daily steam train, with its two carriages, left Buckingham station to travel a few miles westwards through green fields to nearby Brackley, an even smaller town than Buckingham, set on a hillside in the county of Northamptonshire. On the train, Jan joined a group of 'day boys', so called by comparison with those 'boarders' who lived at the school for the duration of each of the year's three academic terms. The road from Brackley station led uphill, past a market hall, to widen into a long market square, which continued further upwards before becoming road again. On one of the full sides of the square stretched the stone and brick walls of buildings, forming the public face of Magdalen College School. The school chapel dominated the highest level of the site. Nearby, a pair of cast-iron gates allowed glimpses of dormitory and classroom blocks forming courtyards and of a sports pavilion, beyond which playing fields stretched into the distance.

For Jan, the weeks of that first winter term were fast filled with experiences so new, so different, so layered on top of his father's death and his mother's absence. Alongside his known familiar school subjects of English and Mathematics, he now found himself being taught History, Geography, Physics, Chemistry, French, Latin, Art and Religious Studies, each taught by a different teacher and often in different locations of classroom, laboratory or studio.

Teachers' academic roles were often supplemented by their other school responsibilities. The headmaster, the Revered Morton, considered himself to be the natural and logical dispenser of Religious Studies. Mr Ritter, the Physics tutor, coached the first fifteen rugby team as well as cross-country running. He also supervised swimming lessons in the school's algae-ridden pool. Mr Ballard, the Maths tutor, coached the first eleven cricket team. Mr Trent, the English tutor, who had the most recent military experience among the staff, commanded the school's Army Cadet Force. Mr Humbold, a violently patriotic man, was in charge of History, Geography and the school Debating Society. Mr Spencer, the Latin tutor, a bald-headed man with an aquiline nose whom the boys called 'JC' because of his supposed resemblance to Julius Caesar, was in charge of the film society. His choices of hired sixteen-millimetre Sunday-night films of subversively exciting themes made him the boys' favourite academic. Noticeable among such male-oriented staff was Mrs Morton, the Chemistry tutor, a haughty woman who believed that her status as the headmaster's wife allowed her licence to give orders throughout the school. She only retained the boys' respect by encouraging them to conduct experiments which would produce noisy explosions in the lab, though her other responsibilities, those of school catering and the supervision of groups tending the school allotments, added only few further admirers.

Music was not highlighted in the school. The elderly Mr Denman, 'Jimmy' to the boys, administered a programme of visiting instrumentalists who taught individual aspiring musicians. Jan chose to learn to play the piano, for which teaching was undertaken by Mr Denman himself, but at an early stage of progress Jan became aware that his teacher often fell asleep in mid-chord, so lessons were no longer taken.

Art was pursued only in out-of-school hours. Boys were keen to sign up for sessions, partly because it was possible to 'let go' with paper and water and paints and splurging colours, partly because the often-unsupervised art studio was located close to the tuck shop by the playing fields, away from the main school buildings. 'Nobby' Giles, the tuck shop manager and school general factotum, was the boys' friend in all matters, prepared to sell out-of-hours sweets and drinks at low prices.

The second dominant female among the staff was Mrs Mackenzie, addressed only as 'Matron', a confident Scotswoman to whom all turned for advice and cure when illness struck. Matron's sickbay ward, which she ruled with firmness and understanding, was appreciated by all as a haven of rest and recuperation.

Jan remained a 'day boy' until the end of term. On each school day evening, he and his latest friends would retake the train to home stations back along the line. On arrival at Buckingham station, impelled by hunger, Jan would cover the short distance to the Jones household in quick time. The house was always warm, with open coal fires burning in the hearths of the living and dining rooms and in Reverend Jones's study.

Mrs Jones would always welcome Jan with, "Hello, my dear, supper's cooking; you must be hungry; we'll eat soon," an expectation soon fulfilled by a tasty three course meal. Time between supper and bed was spent quietly in the living room. Mrs Jones liked reading. Her husband would join her or would disappear into his study to prepare a sermon. Jan often had homework to complete.

Miss Shuttleworth, deep in her armchair, would wait impatiently for him to be free. At that given moment, she would interpose: "Jan, do come over. And do bring a stool."

Then, bible-reading study would begin. During the day, Miss Shuttleworth had always prepared two or three passages from the old or new testaments. From these, she would now read quietly to the boy before offering explanations, making connections, asking him questions to which he would reluctantly respond, but for her sake rather than his own. The sessions would usually end on the intervention of Mrs Jones: "Elizabeth, my dear, don't forget that Jan has been at school all day and will be up again early in the morning."

The Christmas holidays of 1941 reunited mother and son. Ilona was living in a single room in the Old Beams, a boarding house located on Aylesbury market square.

"You have your own room," Ilona said. "The building is three hundred years old, very romantic and what is called higgledy-piggledy. We, all the residents, eat our meals in the ground-floor public restaurant. About twenty people live here; they are all so interesting. One is a doctor, another a newspaper reporter, another a solicitor, like me they all work in this county town – you will like them!"

Over Christmas, the Old Beams restaurant was always closed to the public. The boarding-house guests decorated a main ground room in readiness for their own meals and festivities. Then, as a family of friends of all ages, they ate, drank and let themselves go. Jan liked the games, especially 'Murder', where he threw himself into whatever role the cards predicted for him, whether murderer, detective or victim. The Elizabethan passages and dark hiding places of the building, the creaking of floorboards and beams, made perfect backgrounds for his enthusiasm.

One of the guests, Bill, a reporter with the *Bucks Herald*, became Jan's mentor, teaching him to gamble at cards with 'Twenty-One', which fast became the boy's obsession. Bill confessed to Ilona: "Just a numbers game, really, it's good for Jan's mathematics skills, and we're only betting with match sticks. Mind you, might also teach him that sometimes in life he'll have to take chances and maybe lose…"

For the remainder of December and into the new year, one of Jan's friends from school, William Ballard, joined him at the Old Beams. Ilona was at work. Each day, she allocated pocket money to the two boys. "This is for sandwiches and drinks at lunchtime in the British Restaurant."

The boys roamed the town all day, setting up rowdy adventures in streets, parks and playgrounds. On one occasion, they slipped, unnoticed, too young and without paying, into the cinema to watch a horror film starring Boris Karloff, whose sliding gait and outstretched arms they later enjoyed impersonating. The local Odeon was also a draw for the Saturday Morning Cinema Club, where they could see Gene Autry, or Roy Rogers and Trigger, or *Flash Gordon's Trip to Mars* with the hateful Emperor Ming.

In mid-January, Ilona received a letter from the Czech government-in-exile.

"Jan, Jan, President Beneš's committee want to pay for you to live at school in term time."

"So I won't be able to stay with the Reverend and Mrs Jones?"

"No, dear, I'm so sorry, but you will always be able to visit them and they will always remain our friends."

In that January of 1942, snow covered the buildings and landscape of his Northamptonshire school. Jan, the new boarder, was allocated a bed in a twelve-boy dormitory located over the headmaster's study. 'Lights out and no talking' was a rule strictly enforced at 9.00pm. The blankets were heavy and cosy. He slept well as always.

So began a further eight-year period of schooling in which a boy from middle Europe, from part of a distant Austro-Hungarian Empire, would be nurtured within the traditions of a minor English public school, perhaps to become an Englishman.

In the school library, a singular sense of history was often made clear to the boys by the florid Mr Humbold. "Look at your maps, see how about a quarter of the world is coloured in red… we talk of the 'all-red routes', first mapped by English explorers like Cecil Rhodes. Then, the English became instrumental in developing all those lands, setting up order via workable systems of administration and government. When we've won the war, I hope that such a tradition will be carried on by boys like yourselves!"

But it was to Mr Humbold's credit, in the later war years of 1942 to 1945, that he made his pupils aware of a wider world undergoing ever more violent conflict and change. Cecil Rhodes became a shadow of the past. Instead would come explanations about places, people and events parallel to the boys' own lives: in 1942 Stalingrad, El Alamein and Singapore; in '43 North Africa and Burma; in '44 Anzio, Monte Cassino and Normandy.

In the early evening of the 6th of June 1944, when the boarders were eating their combined tea and supper, they were surprised to see the Reverend Morton burst into the dining room. He was excited, an unusual state for him. "Boys. Do listen, all of you. Some of you may already have heard wireless announcements that today is a historic day. Our military forces, together with those of our allies, have landed on the French Normandy coast to commence the invasion of Western Europe. We will take back the countries occupied by Hitler's Germany. The war is turning in our favour. No doubt we will learn more over the coming days."

Some days later, Jan received a letter from his mother.

"Jan, my dear, you will have heard and read about the news of the invasion. If only your father could have been here. He would have been so happy. I am only sad when I think how many more people will have to die before this is all over.

Your loving mother, Ilona."

Mr Humbold's lessons continued to illuminate the daily announcements of fighting and struggle: 1944 included Sicily, Eastern Europe, Paris, Berlin, Dresden and Guam; '45 began with a name which would remain seared into the boys' later manhoods. That name was Auschwitz.

On the morning of Tuesday 8th May 1945, shortly into the start of the summer term, all lessons were halted as the Reverend Morton called for a school gathering in the main hall. As soon as the boys were assembled, he made his announcement:

"Boys, you may already have seen or heard the commotion out on Brackley town square, and some of the day boys will have heard the radio bulletins… and it has been confirmed and yes, it has happened at last… the war in Europe has ended. The Germans signed surrender documents yesterday at two in the morning, so today is VE, Victory in Europe Day… amazing, amazing, the Prime Minister is due to speak to us on the radio at three o'clock this afternoon… already there are huge gatherings all over the country, huge rejoicings in London, crowds at Buckingham Palace, dancing and singing…"

He wiped his eyes hurriedly.

"There will be no further lessons today. The day boys may wish to return home to be with their families. On the other hand, they are welcome to rejoice here with us all… we will have a special lunch which Mrs Morton is organising, we will all gather here in the Main Hall again at two fifty in readiness for Mr Churchill's broadcast to the nation at three, after which we are all invited to join in a teatime Brackley street party, which is even now starting to be prepared in the town square."

The events of that day developed beyond the boys' expectations. The boarders were allowed to receive phone calls from their parents. Nobby Giles was instructed to sell tuck shop provisions at reduced prices. The Prime Minister's radio address confirmed his pugnacious leadership qualities and earned three cheers in the Main Hall. The town's street party began in mid-afternoon. The buildings around the square were festooned in flags and coloured bunting. Crowds ate and drank, sang and danced, embraced and kissed, much to the enjoyment of the Magdalen boys and the local high school girls. The festivity continued well into the night, well beyond the moment when the boarders were induced to return to their dormitories and until such time in the early morning of 9th May when all of Brackley's hostelries had run dry.

A week after VE day, Jan received a letter from his mother:

"My dear son,

You and your school friends and your teachers will all have been celebrating the end of that terrible war which has destroyed so many thousands of lives. Thank goodness it is all over. Of course, I have been thinking a lot about your father. If only he had lived to see this! Though, he always believed that the right end would come. Uncle Franticek has contacted me. He sends you greetings and love. His army unit is being demobilised and he intends to return to Prague. He says that he will join the foreign service in a government which will be led by President Beneš who is returning from exile. 'A new government for a new Czechoslovakia,' he says, he is so optimistic, just as your father always was. He asks if we will also return. I told him no, I think we will not go back, but said that I would ask you, of course. Do you agree with my thinking? You are at school here now, your friends are here, you speak more English than you ever spoke Czech or German and you are also learning French. You will soon have lived more years in this country than in our old homeland, which will have changed forever. You are likely to have only four or five more years of schooling, all still paid by the Czech government, before applying to university, or will be starting to earn your living in this wonderful country which has protected us.

Write to me when you have time. With all my love. Mother."

There were no alternatives for Jan. He wrote back to his mother to say that he wanted to stay, to move forward here. For the remainder of the summer term, he continued to involve himself in every possible school activity, from long, energetic hours on the cricket field to shorter, concentrated hours in the classroom, where he was specially enjoying the English Language, English Literature and Latin classes. Mr Humbold's History lessons were also full of interest because he always began by talking about what was at that moment happening in the world.

"Let's not only be enthusiastic about Europe," he would remind the senior boys. "I'm sure that all your lives will develop differently because of our victory. But don't forget that we and our Commonwealth forces and our American allies are still fighting the Japanese in the Far East."

Over the remainder of the term, Mr Humbold's discussions with his pupils often referred to the three great allied war leaders: Churchill, Stalin and Roosevelt. Latterly, the name of a new American president, Harry S Truman, began to be known. It was in school summer vacation time that this name would echo around the world, when it was learnt that President Truman had ordered two atomic bombs to be dropped, for the first time in history, on two Japanese cities. On 6th August 1945, the first bomb, called 'Little Boy', was dropped on the city of Hiroshima. 140,000 people died instantly. On 9th August, the second bomb, called 'Fat Man', was dropped on the city of Nagasaki. Some 74,000 people died instantly.

In the afternoon of 14th August, radio bulletins announced that Japan's Emperor Hirohito had offered his country's unconditional surrender. Formal confirmation followed on the fifteenth, when the world began to celebrate VJ (Victory over Japan) Day, the day which finally ended the whole of the Second World War.

Back at school, in a late 1945 autumn term history lesson, Mr Humbold reminded his senior class of some vital statistics.

"This Second World War has been the biggest armed conflict in history. In Europe, about fifty million people have been killed, including some fifteen million soldiers, twenty million Russian civilians and six million Jews."

He tried to continue calmly.

"On the other side of the world, in Asia and the Far East, about a further thirty million people have been killed, including some seven million soldiers and twenty-five million civilians. If that terrible atomic bombing had not taken place, it is reckoned that the war would have continued for a further two years, in which millions more soldiers and civilians on all sides would have died. Thankfully it is all over, though we also have to remember that thousands more may yet continue to become ill and to die as a result of the atomic bombings. The world has not known such warfare before. I just hope that your generation will never see the like of it again. The world would destroy itself."

On a following week, Mr Humbold decided to add to one of his normal class lessons. "Boys," he started, "wars or no wars, have you ever considered why the traditions of the English public school have followed their own steady course, with academic paths supported by extra-curricular objectives? Here are a few of those objectives which you might think about…

"Sportsmanship and fair play should be inculcated on the school's playing fields. Hierarchies of attainment at third, second or first levels, whether at rugby or cricket, should develop an aspiration for success, an aim for fitness. Winning games against other public schools should be considered highly important, a mark of the school's standing equal to academic achievement.

"Leadership, responsibility and teamwork should be encouraged by membership of groups, perhaps beginning with cubs and scouts, often leading to the army cadet force with its drilling, shooting and joint summer exercises with our national soldiers."

With the briefest glance at the ceiling, Mr Humbold

added, "It would be considered essential that these building blocks are assembled within an overriding framework of faith and discipline… for which our headmaster Reverend Morton considers himself responsible above all others."

The boys were well aware of the head's routine! Every Sunday in term time, Charles Morton officiated at the 11.00am matins and 6.00pm evensong Church of England services in the school chapel. Usually, he preached the morning sermon, though sometimes he afforded that opportunity to a local Brackley curate. All school boarders were expected to attend. Brackley townspeople were also welcome, though those who came did so more to delight in the chapel's stained-glass windows than to the copybook content of the reverend's sermons.

On weekdays, the headmaster, beyond discharging purely administrative duties, would become livelier in his role as ultimate arbiter of school discipline. "Boys have naughty dispositions," he would observe to anyone who listened. "And verbal admonition makes little impact." He found more favour in the use of the cane, becoming well-known for dispensing 'six of the best', which he applied with vigour, making a diagonal half-run across his study with the familiar raised bamboo, which would fall on the posterior of a 'naughty' culprit who had been positioned to bend over the high back of a chair in the opposite corner of the room. A boy so punished carried his marks of distinction with pride. Jan too was among such bands of heroes, but for deeds long afterwards forgotten.

As teen-age took over the boys' development, all matters of schooling, academic or other, became affected by bodily growth. Fights were common and on the whole were friendly. Bullying, mental or physical, was not uncommon, even if only a particular pastime of particular boys. One such boy, remembered by others well into their manhood, was Henry Bilson. Henry's tactics were to issue a 'friendly wrestling' challenge to another boy. In the course of the fight, Henry would work to throw his opponent to the ground. There, he would proceed to render the opponent immobile by sitting on his thighs while also kneeling on his arms. With the opponent now facing skyward, Henry would proceed to rain heavy blows into the upturned head, eyes, nose and mouth beneath. The hammering would continue until an opponent's yells, or a rescuing boy, or Henry's inclination, would put a stop to the proceedings.

Henry was disliked by all for his bullying, but this did not stop him seeking out new victims. When Jan first became a boarder, he was latest in line for the Bilson treatment. Fortunately, any member of London's Bees gang had learnt to fight. Within a moment of Henry's unexpected first punch, Jan was able to push sideways out of the initial grip, then to throw a heavy counterpunch, upon which the bully immediately withdrew. Jan's hero rating was strengthened.

To boys in their early teens, the importance of fighting was overtaken by thoughts and feelings about girls. There was the magnet of the all-girls high school in the town, towards which the day boys in particular could drift on their way home after lessons had ended at 4.00pm. Fruitful liaisons were established. The boarders were jealous but nevertheless devised complex schemes to compensate for their disadvantage. The best night-time ventures included a group escape out of dormitory windows via knotted bed sheets, then the scaling of the school gates, a run across the dimly lit town square, further scaling of the nearby high school gates, a prising open of windows alongside the senior girls' classroom, a searching of desks to establish named ownerships and then, triumph and bliss, the penknifed carving of a boy's and girl's initials, forever sunk into the desk's wooden lid, together with a handwritten note inside the desk hopefully setting up a future meeting.

Such a mission's return runs and climbs were easy. Less pleasing would be the next day's repercussions, when the high school headmistress's complaints to the Reverend Morton would inevitably lead to an enquiry and the caning session of a whole group, with Jan sometimes among them. Jan wondered if perhaps the headmaster might also be a little pleased that his boys were already working together so well in teams.

In the Aylesbury boarding house at the start of the summer holidays, Jan heard the lodgers discussing each of their own post-war plans for the future. Some intended to move back to London. One couple had decided to be married. Ilona's friend Bill had applied for a job with the *Manchester Guardian*. Ilona herself told Jan of her intention to seek promotion in Aylesbury's central dental clinic. There was excitement for national change. Jan heard his mother's friends talking loudly about an 'election' in which each had just recently 'voted'.

"I could not vote," his mother said. "Because we are not English yet. My friends argue so much. Some want the Conservative Party and Mr Churchill, our great wartime

Prime Minister, to be in charge of the country even now in the new peacetime. Others want a Mr Attlee and his Labour Party to take charge. Bill was hoping that you would be here to help him distribute leaflets for Mr Attlee."

On the morning of Thursday 26th July, Jan and Ilona were breakfasting when Bill burst into the public dining room. "We've done it! Landslide! We've done it! The returning soldiers, sailors and airmen have done it! Now watch to see our new social programmes for health and employment and pensions!" The words kept pouring out. Jan wondered when Bill would eat his shredded wheat.

By early September, Jan was ready to go back to Brackley at the start of another school year. Whenever he had begun to make friends on holiday, it soon became time to say goodbye. He now felt surrounded by the grown-ups of the Old Beams. Aylesbury had become almost dull. Consolation had arrived in the form of a summer fair, which had been laid out in rural surroundings on the town's northern boundary. For a whole week of afternoons and evenings, the fair burst into action, with crowds hungry for pleasure among the colour and noise of stalls, swings, roundabouts and a large carousel. Would-be cowboys tested their sharpshooting at the rifle stall, would-be he-men tested their strengths at the sledgehammer stall… while seekers after destiny offered their hands to Madame Divina the Palmist.

Jan prepared to increase the value of his pocket money at the penny-rolling stall, challenging each penny to roll down its wooden groove towards a square in which the coin had to rest without touching any edge lines. He learnt much: as with life, sometimes you win, sometimes you lose. At the moment when his pennies had all gone, he became aware of a girl who had been standing beside him, following his moves carefully.

"Have you lost it all?" she asked.

"Yes… it doesn't matter."

"Will you try again tomorrow?"

"Yes. Will you be here?"

"I could be."

He liked the way she looked.

"What's your name?" he asked.

"June. My brothers call me Juney… it's a bit silly."

"It's alright. I'm Jan. Do you want to walk around a bit?"

"If you like."

They walked together in the crowd. He was more aware of her than of the surroundings. When they came to the shooting stall he said, "I'll try this tomorrow."

"Oo!" she said, and laughed. "That would be good!"

He liked the easy way that she laughed.

"Meet you just here then, tomorrow, about the same time?"

"Yes," she said.

Next day, he was first to arrive and joined the stall queue. She appeared at his elbow just as he was being handed a rifle over the counter. The entrance fee paid for three bullets. His aim was steady and his pressure on the trigger was careful and controlled. The bullseye target was centrally shattered, no problem for an army cadet. The stallholder waved his arms over the prizes.

"Choose what you want, young man… any one thing off the shelf."

Jan the cadet made a military left turn to his companion. "What would you like?"

June did not hesitate. She pointed to a small brown teddy bear which she then clutched eagerly.

With a free hand, she held Jan's arm and pulled him forwards through the fairground. He followed easily, surprised to see her so animated. In no time, they reached the quiet of open fields and farmland. She walked fast, as if in search, still pulling him until, on a higher stretch of meadow she released his arm, threw herself down on her back and, still holding the bear to her chest, looked up at Jan. Uncertain, he knelt down next to her. She pulled him closer and kissed him. She was warm. He liked this. She pulled her summer dress over her head and threw it on the grass. She took both his hands and moved them slowly and with pressure over all parts of her body. He responded, feeling pleasure. He could tell from her movements that she was pleased, too. So, they stayed, growing to know each other, until the sun was fading. As they walked away, unhurried now, he wondered about the teddy bear… perhaps he too had liked the afternoon.

"See you tomorrow, same time, same stall?" he asked before they parted. He thought that she nodded.

On the next day, the last day of the holiday, June did not appear. Jan waited through the afternoon, before going home to pack his suitcase for school. *I don't even have her address*, he thought. *I wonder how old she was.* He thought back to Naďa in Prague. *Naďa was my angel. June was so real.*

The autumn term of 1945 set in motion Jan's final four years in the senior course of Magdalen College School. In those years, his friendships, his academic studies and his sporting activities all intensified. School life was steady. For him, this quiet Northamptonshire town was an anchor. His mother kept in touch by letter writing:

"I was given that job," she wrote in October. "I'm going to be the chief dental nurse for Buckinghamshire. Your father would be teasing me… 'All those languages, all those Freud lectures, all that degree,' he would be saying. Never mind. The people with whom I work are lovely. I can now also rent a small, thatched cottage which I've seen in a village near Aylesbury. You will be able to help me paint the walls. You could also help me dig the garden, which I have to tell you is heavy clay! But you are strong."

A November letter followed shortly after:

"František has written to tell me that in October, President Beneš gave a now-famous speech to his Provisional Assembly. Your uncle has sent me a whole copy of the speech. Here is the first sentence: 'Today we, the Czechoslovak nation, are again standing with all our moral strength in our own free Prague.' Good, isn't it? Franto is so proud to be part of what he says is the only European government which has returned from exile after the war."

Jan found his yearly school and holiday involvements increasing in intensity. At school, he was promoted in stages to reach the first eleven cricket team and the first fifteen rugby team. In the army cadet force, he was given Corporal's stripes. He also joined the school's Dramatic Society and played the part of Chorus in a production of *Henry V*. In history classes, Mr Humbold looked to enlist his comments when worldwide news was discussed.

At holiday times, he helped Ilona set up her latest home in the rented thatched cottage. On the long wall of the single ground-floor room, he painted a rich, yellow colour, which his mother completed by hanging a full-sized print of a favourite painting: Picasso's 'Child with Dove'. In good weather, he helped to dig the cottage garden to assist his mother's planting programme, which produced all-year-round fruit and vegetables. Once, in the summer of 1946, he allowed himself to revisit that year's Aylesbury annual fair. But there was no June. Nor were there any clues of her.

At a cottage breakfast during the Easter holiday of 1947, Ilona opened a brown envelope marked 'Home Office'. With a burst of breath, she was able to make a joyful announcement to Jan: "We have received our naturalisation papers. We are both English now."

The regularity of Jan's school life was interrupted by a letter from his mother in the spring of 1948:

"Dear boy," she wrote. "I know that we will soon be seeing each other at Easter, but there is some sad news which you should know now. Mr Humbold might have told your class how Russia has forced a so-called 'coup' on the Czech government in Prague. In February, a new prime minister, Gottwald, and other Communists, were appointed to serve under President

Beneš, who could not stop this. Then, on 10ᵗʰ March, our much-loved foreign minister, Jan Masaryk, was said to have killed himself by jumping out of a third-floor window at the Prague foreign office. I and many others can only believe that he was pushed but, because Russia is probably involved, this will never be proved. But, sadly, more. I have just received a letter from the Czech Embassy in London. The details tell how your dear uncle did not want to live under the new regime. Of his own free will, he jumped from the same balcony. I am so, so sorry.

Franta loved you so much. We will talk more when you come home.

With many hugs,
Mother."

The Easter holidays were quiet. Ilona tried to open up discussions, but Jan showed little inclination to talk. Instead, he now more regularly opened his chess set box. Then, with František's present – the Niemzowitsch Chess Praxis – by his side for a few hours each day, he began gradually to understand the place notations and to play master moves from some of the world's famous chess games which were recorded in the book.

Ilona understood that her son would never forget his uncle.

Summer brought further mixed news. In June, his mother wrote to tell him that President Beneš had resigned.

"He must be ill," she guessed. *"Trying to be the leader of a system now run by Russia."*

By contrast, English news bulletins on the morning of 5th July were full of optimism: a new National Health Service was being opened for every man, woman and child. Ilona had again written: "*Any person who becomes ill will be able to receive medical treatment without having to pay. We are citizens of a socialist country of which your father would have been so proud.*"

Further July news, personal for Jan, came from the headmaster's office. Inside an envelope was a thick sheet of paper titled 'University of Oxford School Certificate'. The details revealed three 'Very Good's for English Language, English Literature and Latin; five 'Credit's for History, Religious Knowledge, French, Mathematics and Art; and a 'Pass' for Science. A note from the headmaster was also attached, with the words '*Well done, Dusek*' written with flourish and signed '*C. Morton*'. The results were celebrated at a summer holiday tea party in the Aylesbury Old Beams, to which a circle of former lodgers and friends specially returned.

On a tranquil early September evening, still in holiday time, Ilona returned to the cottage with the news that President Beneš had died. "It is not clear from what illness," she said. "I guess a broken heart. How would he want to live on when our country is once again under foreign oppression? But it is no longer our country, is it? We are here, looking forwards, not backwards." Then came an afterthought: "Although, I am now going to cook us a backwards-looking supper of red cabbage and apple…"

The last week of the summer vacation was timetabled in the school calendar as the Army Cadet Force Annual Training Week. Jan joined twenty of the senior boys, all, like him, aged around sixteen, at an army camp in the west of England. They were accompanied by Mr Trent, dressed in his former army captain's uniform. The first few days after arrival included sessions for kitting out, gymnasium work, parade-ground drilling and shooting. Through midweek, the party took part in preparatory talks prior to the main training event: the night exercise, which finally arrived.

As darkness fell, the cadets with rifles and equipment were shepherded onto the open backs of two 'one-ton' army lorries. It was standing-room only. Exciting. The lorry drivers, regular soldiers, took off at speed into the west country. In the leading lorry, Jan and his close friend, William, their arms stretched high to grip the steel-framed roof structure, were standing alongside the lorry's forward open edge, from which they could just see the back of the driver's neck as he swung the vehicle through a landscape of narrow lanes, hedges and trees. The tightly packed prospective soldiers shouted joyfully to each other. The driver, seemingly unaware of a misty darkness ahead, continued to swerve the vehicle faster around lane bends as if in response to the prevailing glee. Then, a front left-hand-side wheel slipped into a lane-side ditch and the whole lorry somersaulted onto its roof, with Jan, William and others thrown into the night sky.

On the following day, Jan awoke in a military hospital. He could just see Mr Trent by the side of the bed.

"Don't try to speak," Mr Trent was saying. "It will be painful; your jaw is broken and your face resembles a pumpkin."

Jan could make out others in beds around the ward. He mumbled, "William?"

After a hesitation, Mr Trent said, "I am sorry, your good friend is no longer with us. He was thrown under the lorry bonnet. He must have been killed instantly."

The Reverend Morton preached his best at a memorial service in the school chapel when the new academic year began. William's parents, who had flown in from South America, were there, as was his older sister from the Wrens, also his younger brother who had not yet joined the cadet force. Ilona was among all parents of the boys who had ridden on the two lorries. All consoled each other, aware that broken bones would heal but that William was gone.

The school routine continued as always. The rugby fixtures, home or away, fitted dates which had been planned a year before. The choir began weekly practice months ahead of the annual scheduled Christmas carol service. The sixth formers were set programmes of study to suit their chosen examinations, still two years away. Mr Trent had chosen an English Literature syllabus for Jan, whom he was recommending for a scholarship to Magdalen College Oxford. In addition, he thought to test and extend the knowledge and understanding of his literature group by pinning poetry quotations onto the sixth form classroom door each Friday lunchtime, then calling for the authors' names and poem titles to be discovered by the start of the following week.

"As well as answers, anyone can add a poem of their own, if they so wish," Mr Trent suggested.

On a particular Friday, close to the end of term, the sixth form door revealed three quotations. The first read:

"Life is real! Life is earnest!
and the grave is not its goal;
'Dust thou art, to dust returnest'
was not spoken of the soul."

The second read:

"I strove with none, for none was worth my strife;
Nature I loved, and next to Nature, Art;
I warmed both hands beside the fire of Life;
It sinks; and I am ready to depart."

The third read:

"I believe in Michelangelo, Velasquez, and Rembrandt;
in the might of design, the mystery of colour,
the redemption of all things by Beauty everlasting,
and the message of Art that has made these hands blessed.
Amen. Amen."

Student detective searches in the library's reference books and poetry anthologies provided answers, duly pinned up by classmates on Monday morning. The consensus was:

1. Henry Wadsworth Longfellow. 'Voices of the Night'.
2. Walter Savage Landor. 'Dying Speech of an Old Philosopher'.
3. George Bernard Shaw. 'The Doctor's Dilemma'.

Jan volunteered an addition of his own, which read:

*"We carry our deaths with us
when we come and go.
Why do others add more?"*

At the Monday morning class discussion, which usually followed such submissions, Mr Trent proceeded gently. Perhaps he knew that he had pushed too far.

"Jan," he asked, "do you have a title for your poem?"

"I was thinking of 'They Keep Coming'. But it could just be 'Why?'."

Mr Trent chose to move the class on to the general Literature syllabus.

1949 turned out to be Jan's last year of schooling. He became a substitute elder brother to Mason, the younger Ballard, a friendship which would last a lifetime. He furthered his interest in the cinema when asked by Mr Spencer to assist in choosing films for the boarders' Sunday-evening film club. He pursued his sixth form English literature syllabus with energy and wonder. He joined in the weekly current affairs discussions which Mr Humbold had set up as an extra-mural event in the library. All that year of '49, Mr Humbold centred on 'Aspects of Communism': how Russia had reluctantly opened the Berlin blockade, how Russia had tested its first atomic bomb, how Russia's belligerence had obliged twelve 'western' nations to form a new defensive military alliance: the North Atlantic Treaty Organisation (NATO), and how, in October on the other side of the world, a new

Communist nation, the People's Republic of China, had just been formed by a new leader.

"Except he calls himself 'Chairman'," Mr Humbold said. "Chairman Mao Tse Tung. Who knows what economic and social plans he has for his own people, the largest nation in the world. Will he be as ruthless as 'comrade' Stalin has been to his own Russian citizens, killed in the Gulag labour camps? What is this all leading to? We've just finished one war. Will there be further wars in your lifetimes? And will other leaders of many of the world's nations again have total power over their own people?"

As if to reinforce his declamation, Mr Humbold reminded the boys: "On 8th June, a new novel was published which you should all read. The author is George Orwell. The book is titled *1984*."

It was at a mid-year meeting with Mr Spencer, with whom Jan was helping to choose a future batch of films for hiring, that Mr S (by then just 'JC' on friendship terms) said, "Jan, *The Times* newspaper has published invitations for people who may want to study for top careers in the British film industry. Two- or three-year studentships are available, with pay, but will be dependent on interviews. Would you be interested? I know how cinema fascinates you, but then I also know how the school is pointing you towards a Literature scholarship at Oxford."

Against the combined advice of Reverend Morton, Mr Trent and of Ilona, Jan wrote for the necessary application forms on which he stated that he wished to become a film art director. He then submitted the forms to the J Arthur Rank Organisation, Denham Film Studios, Buckinghamshire.

After a long waiting period, he was called for an interview. A day away from school brought him to Denham Studios, a township of buildings, hangers and sheds, and the discarded settings of streets depicting far-flung places. He was directed to an interview room where a man and a woman welcomed him and engaged him in friendly conversation.

"Why art direction?" they wanted to know.

Jan tried to explain: "I like films so much; they tell us so much about life. The backgrounds to stories are so important; what they look like has to be right."

He wasn't sure if he was explaining properly, but they went on questioning: "Do you like drawing?"

Jan opened a small folio of his school art class drawings.

His interviewers seemed particularly to appreciate his pencil sketch of Magdalen College School's medieval chapel interior. "Very architectural," they said.

Then it was all over. The woman spoke first: "We would like you to join us. The studentship is for three years. You will often be working side by side with both of us here at Denham, in the design studio. Paul and I will be your teachers, but others will also advise you. Our apologies for the lack of earlier introductions. I am Carmen Dillon, and this is Paul Sheriff. We have each been fortunate in our art direction work, we jointly received Academy Award nominations for Laurence Olivier's *Henry V* and, only last year, I was given the Academy Award for the art direction of Olivier's *Hamlet*."

7

BEFORE CHRISTMAS 1949 Jan left Magdalen College School. He was just seventeen, a public school-educated young Englishman by courtesy of the exiled government of the country of his birth.

In January 1950, Jan began to earn his own living. He was able to rent single-room accommodation in Gerrards Cross, close to Denham, in the home of a Mr and Mrs Poulter, an elderly couple whose children had long since moved on. Mr Poulter owned the town's only shoe shop, to which he went all day, leaving his wife to enjoy meeting friends and preparing evening meals for himself and Jan, who was treated like a long-lost son.

Early each morning, Jan cycled to work. Activity inside the studio gates was often already hectic amid noise and movement of people and vehicles. Groups of extras responded to shouted orders on what appeared to be only half-built backdrops. By contrast, peace reigned inside the design studio, where Carmen and Paul sometimes appeared to have been drawing all night. They would still find time daily to involve Jan in the film on which each or both were working. More often it was Carmen who would show him how the sketch artist's postage-stamp diagrams could be turned into constructible sets made from timber, or how he could combine the use of drawing instruments with his own freehand instinctive drawing techniques, or how he could use fixed camera angle measurements to distort the layout of a set in order to compensate between what the camera shoots and what the eye sees. Each day would bring varied activities: the completion of a drawing for a set, the visit to the carpenters' workshops to check or discuss set construction, the late-morning visit to a cinema showing of the previous day's filming, those 'rushes' over which the whole team of director, designers, camera people, actors and all involved would then express contentment or would be prepared to reshoot. If all was well, then team members might hastily talk and eat together in the canteen before moving on to more afternoon filming.

Jan learnt fast. Over a period of two years, he was given increasing design opportunities as he became involved with the making of at least five films, some of which were the responsibility of other art directors, such as the well-known Alex Vetchinsky, who gave Jan the task of designing the sailors' bunk room in a John Mills submarine saga *Morning Departure*. Alex would never accept Jan's initial designs but would smudge his large fingers and thumbs over the drawing details to indicate improvements needed. A new drawing would then have to be made. Another of Jan's sets was a successful canopied railway station platform for the film *Trio*, a collection of three Somerset Maugham short stories.

The starlet, Jean Simmons, was about Jan's age. When she sat next to him to view the previous day's 'rushes', he had eyes only for her.

The most powerful set, on which Jan worked with a team, was in a film titled *Give Us This Day* or alternatively, *Christ in Concrete*, the story of an Italian immigrant bricklayer who falls to his death on a New York building site. Many drawings were produced for the high tenement-like structure. Many rushes were seen and rejected by the director, Edward Dmytryk, who was admired and supported by the whole film crew for his attention to detail. Dmytryk had newly arrived in England, having fled America after being denounced as a communist and blacklisted for 'Un-American Activities'. On days when the rushes were deemed to be a success, Dmytryk and the team, including a fellow American, actor Sam Wanamaker, would allow themselves relaxation time and conversation in the canteen. Jan would listen with rapt attention to accounts of Senator McCarthy's witch-hunt trials, which were still then ongoing.

"I will stay in England," Wanamaker announced. "To act here and perhaps build a new Shakespeare theatre in London."

One day in late 1950, Carmen and Paul asked Jan to join them for a discussion. Unusually, it was Paul who began.

"There's trouble ahead, Jan, for this great film industry of ours. Our boss and business leader, Mr J Arthur Rank, whose fortune in flour milling was funding all we do, is pulling back on his support for productions at Denham and Pinewood. Maybe the studios will revive in a year or two, but right now Carmen and I and you and all our team are about to lose our jobs at the end of the month. You were progressing well. We wonder how we might help you to decide on a way forward."

Jan showed no sign of being troubled. "What do you think I should do?"

"You may know that Carmen and I are both architects which is helpful to our work here. You, too, could consider studying to become an architect. Many career paths would open for you."

Jan made enquiries. An overall five-year full-time architecture course was too expensive for someone like himself, who had no savings. But there was an available route: one could study part-time for five years on a London architectural night-school course, while working daytime hours in an architect's office to gain practical experience and a living salary. This would lead to partial qualification, on the basis of which a student could gain government funding to study full-time for a further two years.

Mr and Mrs Poulter willed him on: "We know of an architect who has a small office in London. He might employ you as an apprentice if you are also attending night school. You could continue to live here with us and commute by rail each day."

More enquiries were made. The Poulters' architect friend confirmed that he could indeed take on a junior. The well-established architectural night school at the Northern Polytechnic had vacancies at first year level. So, the scene was set.

Thomas Tomlin was a Quaker who commuted to London each mid-morning from his home in Jordans. Jan was supposed to arrive earlier, particularly in winter, in order to lay and light two coal fires which were to be burning brightly before Mr T was due to arrive at the basement floor of his property in central South Kensington. One other architect, a qualified man, completed the staff numbers. Office jobs included new-build and refurbishment work of a small contract nature. Jan's first tasks were to set up tracing paper location drawings for a three-storey extension of Foyles bookshop in Manette Street. He worked carefully, drawing with hard- and medium-grade pencils, having made sure that he had washed his hands after the fire lighting. Mr Tomlin was a severe taskmaster who checked work late into each evening so that when Jan arrived next day he would find shading, slashing and comments, in soft pencil, across his efforts. *Perhaps this is the way to learn*, he confided to himself.

It would be necessary, Jan thought, to save time and money by giving up commuting and, instead, by living, studying and working in one place, London itself. He and the Poulters wished each other goodbye amid much hugging and Mrs Poulter's sobs. For a minimal rental payment, Jan found a small attic room under the roof of a rundown terrace house in Well Walk, Hampstead, where the landlady regarded him and her other assorted lodgers with a mixture of neediness and hostility.

8

AS HE HAD planned, Jan spent the next five years studying for, and then passing, the Part One Examination of the Royal Institute of British Architects. Over those years, the combinations of daily life – whether in paid employment, in part-time study or in rented lodgings – changed regularly even as they also increased in momentum. His apprenticeship in the South Kensington basement was followed by a junior assistantship in a Holborn practice specialising in small medical buildings. An increase in salary sufficiently covered his rent and food. He would eat lunchtime sandwiches on a bench in Red Lion Square and buy supplies for a frugal evening meal which he cooked on his room's gas ring. At weekends, he and other newly made student friends would swim in all weathers in the pond at the foot of Hampstead Heath.

Jan had a particular reason for returning to Buckinghamshire on weekends at least once a month. Ilona had become a member of NALGO, the National Association of Local Government Officers, whose families played tennis on NALGO-owned courts. There, Jan liked partnering a pretty, dark curly-haired girl of his own age, Hilary Wilkins, who, though shy, seemed to like his company. The weekend would then also include gardening and odd jobs for Ilona, who had settled into her thatched cottage home in Hulcott village beyond Aylesbury. Sometimes he would return to London late on a Sunday night so that he could first join his mother, who now regularly played the village church organ at evensong.

Architectural study was fascinating. On three evenings and one full day a week, he would take the northern line tube train to Holloway Road Station, from where he would walk to the disarray of Polytechnic buildings. There, a lively class of building designers, many of his own age, were joined by older ex-servicemen and women who wanted to complete studies interrupted by the war. The tutors were supportive. They had been teaching full-time students all day but were still prepared to repeat their lectures and drawing assignments for the evening arrivals. Additional design project work would be set for completion in whatever spare time each student was able to find. Links were rapidly made within design groups or over drawing-board discussions and criticisms. An early exercise for all students was a traditional 'measured drawing' which, in Jan's year, happened to be for the polytechnic main entrance doorway and its surroundings.

When labouring to put this to paper, Jan was approached by an older student: "Please, my measurement understanding is not good. How do you call this inches and feet?"

That question was to begin a life-long friendship between Jan and the questioner, who introduced himself.

He was Romek Kowal, tallish, thin, fair-haired. Over the weeks which followed, Jan was made aware of a life parallel with, but so different from, his own. Romek said that he was Polish, that he had come down to London from Windermere, where he had earlier been flown with other refugees from Prague.

"At Windermere classes, they wanted to teach me to be draftsman. But I wanted to be architect. I left. Now, I have not right education, not right English, not Mathematics. But I learn."

Over the first year of the course, Jan helped Romek with his English grammar studies, as well as with Maths and the calculations needed for Architectural Structures. His friend was hungry for knowledge.

Over further subsequent years, Romek would tell Jan his life story. He was the sole survivor of a large Jewish family living in rural Chodecz in Poland. His father, a former soldier in the Russian Czarist army, owned a timber business. When the Germans overran an already anti-Semitic Poland just before the Second World War, all Jewish life was swept away. Romek and his closest relatives were interned in the Łótź Ghetto. There, in 1940 and 1941, Romek's grandfather and father both died of starvation. Romek's mother and sisters, too weak to survive, were marched off by the Germans. Romek hung on as a worker in the ghetto's metal factory, where a daily helping of thin soup was supplemented by morsels of bread, potato, potato peelings and, sometimes, nettles. Romek and the strongest metal workers were taken to Auschwitz-Birkenau, then later Stutthof, concentration camps. There, he witnessed but survived the horrors of the camps. In February 1945, ahead of the advancing Russian Army, Romek and a 'factory workers' group of prisoners were marched to Dresden by their camp captors. The subsequent Allied firebombing of Dresden allowed Romek to escape.

"My grandmother had told me that I must be strong and live."

Over the years of their friendship, Romek would at times speak frankly about life in the camps.

Jan would ask, "How can you stay so calm when you tell me these things? How can you do it? You are describing some of the greatest evils ever perpetrated in history. Evil which the rest of us have been allowed to bypass, kept at a distance by television, the radio, newspapers…"

"I try to stay calm in the day. I never sleep well; all comes back in my dreams. Also, I paint and draw to release it."

Jan told Romek about Herr Blaufeld and Herr Weiner. "That same evil destroyed them and no doubt their families. And there was a girl in Prague, she and her mother were queuing at Gestapo headquarters for exit visas to Israel. I heard later that they didn't reach their promised land. Sometimes I feel guilty when I think how we were allowed to leave freely while others were held back, so often to be murdered."

The five-year course, combined with ever more responsible office design work, seemed so rapidly to have ended. Jan learnt that his project and examination results qualified for a Major Award, which was given to him by the London County Council. Now, evening classes were at an end and he could instead study full-time for a further final two years and with all subsistence guaranteed. He threw himself forward with enthusiasm. He and his friends encouraged each other to become single-minded, fervent, zealous, modern architects. Jan felt himself becoming drawn forwards as a disciple of the architectural 'greats', like Alvar Aalto, Mies van der Rohe and Le Corbusier, all leaders who were exploring new ways of building for a new age, all who combined the designing of buildings with teaching, publishing and 'preaching'. Gone were to be the styles of the past, such as Victorianism, with its heavy entrance steps and porticos which reflected the voice of authority. Gone was to be escapism into decoration and ornament. All was to have simplicity of form bathed in light. The activities of reading, drawing, listening and looking could now be intensified. In the past, he and his fellow students had made sure to visit new London buildings they admired. There was the Royal Festival Hall completed for the 1951 Festival of Britain. There were two pioneer health centres, the first at Peckham, designed by engineer Owen Williams, with its glass-roofed indoor swimming pool, the second at Finsbury, designed by the émigré Berthold Lubetkin. There were the flats at Highgate called 'Highpoint', also designed by Lubetkin. Now, in long holidays from academia, it was further possible to hitch-hike over to mainland Europe to become immersed in the buildings of their architectural heroes. Even a single trip to France could, on a north–south line, sweep up three masterpieces by Le Corbusier; there was his monastery at La Tourette, his nearby church Notre-Dame du Haut and his 'city-in-a-building': the Unité d'Habitation in Marseille.

The two years of diploma course work – years of reading, lecture attendance, building visits, drawing and designing, making models, grappling with aesthetic theory, structures and construction theory, economics and management theory, making presentations and accepting criticism – all passed in a fraction of time, seemingly over before they had begun. Jan's last project, a drawn thesis with a written report, was for a proposed public library building set within his ideas for the central redevelopment of his mother's hometown of Aylesbury, Buckinghamshire. An external examiner, architect Sir Basil Spence of Coventry Cathedral fame, granted him a distinction for the work.

Jan qualified, yet any haze of success did not immediately lead to practice in an architectural office. His adopted country first wanted her share of him. It was time for two years of National Service. Architects tended to apply for army service, particularly in the Royal Engineers, where activities tended to be helpful for their own future careers.

9

THE FIRST SIX weeks of induction to the English military, generally known as 'square bashing', were thought to be common knowledge, but no rumour or anecdote could ever prepare recruits for their initial experiences. Even on that first arrival day, as their one-ton truck was slowing down to halt on a barracks square, Jan and his colleagues could already hear the bellowing voice of the awaiting sergeant.

"Dahn, dahn, you li'lle girly pfhings! When ahve finished wiv yer, yer muvvers will 'av wished they'd never 'ad yer!"

And, once off the truck and immediately stamping their feet, the recruits 'marked time' to the commands: "Le't-righ'! le't-righ'! Laouder, laouder! Oi'd 'ear more noise from a cat bashin 'is prick on a corrugated i'on roof!"

Remembrance of those weeks of shouting and drilling and punishments, all presumably intended to mould ever-thoughtful individual graduates into unthinking, obeying groups, later became the subjects of remembered jokes.

After induction, those who were architects volunteered for, and were generally accepted to join, a subsection of the

Royal Engineers in which they could train to become land surveyors, often for the purposes of carrying out mapping. For six months in a west of England training camp, they learnt this craft, becoming familiar with measuring instruments including theodolites, playing games with 'star shots' and 'sun shots' to check out exactly where the surveying instrument was located on our earth's surface.

Before being sent abroad, each new soldier had to make one further decision: whether to remain 'in the ranks' or to apply to become an officer, even for the remaining short eighteen months of service. All chose to take the required selection tests.

Jan was sent to attend two days of tests at the Military Academy, Sandhurst. On day one, he found himself at a meeting with a group of six other candidates, all unknown to him and apparently destined for different branches of the army.

A broad-shouldered officer supporting several medals on his chest addressed the six: "You will be glad to know that your application paperwork has been cleared. Over these two days, we now intend to put you through a number of tests. We will test you to destruction. We will find out all about you, including your reactions to challenge, your thinking speeds, your potential leadership skills, your concern for others. So good luck!"

A combination of physical and mental exercises continued through the first day, with the participants often more amused than scared.

"What was all that 'testing to destruction'?" asked one of the group, at a moment when he was expected to order the movement of the whole team, plus a long log of wood from one side of a river to the other within a set timescale. "It's just fun and games."

That first evening their taskmaster returned. "Well done, chaps! Not bad so far! Now tonight, we want each of you to prepare a five-minute lecturette on a subject of your own choosing. Tomorrow morning, each of you will then deliver your subject to an assembled panel. Once again, good luck!"

After supper, the candidates dispersed to prepare their talks. Jan thought that an architectural theme might, in his case, be expected. He decided on shock tactics. He would give them the unexpected. He remembered moments of his student days when he had set aside thoughts of architecture and had chosen, as a change, to read Freud's *Introductory Lectures*, perhaps imagining his mother sitting listening with rapt attention in a Vienna University hall. So now, why not Freud lecture material in a Dusek lecturette?

Next morning, Jan's presentation was the last of the six. A row of four high-ranking officers sat at a table before a small, raised speaker's dais.

The leading officer, a middle-aged colonel, looked up. "Alright then, Dusek. What are you going to tell us?"

"I shall speak about the Interpretation of Dreams."

The four looked surprised.

"Will you indeed? Proceed then."

Jan spoke with conviction, as he imagined Freud would have spoken. In only two minutes, he briefly outlined Freud's Theory of Dreams, highlighting childhood, symbolism and wish fulfilment. In a further two minutes, he gave a random example of a single dream, which he then interpreted. In the final minute, he spoke about Freud's own interpretation uncertainties.

For a moment, the four listeners seemed fixed.

Then, the colonel broke the silence: "Exactly five minutes to the second. Very succinct. Thank you, Dusek. You can now leave us to our discussions."

Soon after lunch, the candidates were summoned to meet the colonel, from whom they learnt that they all had passed the tests and would now become 2nd lieutenants in Her Majesty's Army. All shook hands before preparing to return to their own barracks. As Jan was about to leave, the colonel took him to one side.

"Dusek, could you care to join me in a walk around the parade ground?"

The parade ground was empty. The two men walked in step. Jan waited for the colonel to say something.

Finally: "Dusek, your presentation was most interesting. Have you studied the subject of dreams?"

"No, sir, not really studied, but I used to read Freud as a divergence from architecture."

"Interesting. Interesting. You know, Dusek, I have very strong dreams. Even now, I remember my last night's dream so vividly. If I recount it to you, do you think you could hazard an interpretation?"

Jan paused. There was no getting away.

"Yes, sir, of course."

The colonel's dream description which followed included a scene with a dog, a bicycle and a crowd of laughing onlookers.

Jan hesitatingly interpreted: "Perhaps you know someone special to you who has a dog. The dog in your dreams replaces, represents, that special person whom your mind has hidden away. Freud calls it 'transference'. Perhaps you and the person even cycled together in the past? As for the people laughing, I'm not sure about them."

The colonel's shoulders sagged. "Yes, yes. There is a connection. Thank you, Dusek. I am most grateful."

The two shook hands and parted.

Shortly afterwards, Jan's promotion and posting details were confirmed. He would be the junior officer in charge of a platoon of land surveyors within the 32nd Field Survey Squadron, British Army of the Rhein, based in Rheindahlen, a borough of Mönchengladbach in north-west Germany. The platoon's surveys, covering areas of the country which had been heavily destroyed in the war, would be used to produce new maps.

The posting would begin in three weeks. Just enough time to get married to Hilary, the girl from the tennis courts. She would be in Oxford, studying, while he was away. She would have plenty of vacation time to visit Germany. Now to ask her. If she said yes, then to get her father's permission. Hilary Wilkin's reply was a shy, instant yes. Her father's reaction was also a yes, but more carefully considered, more drawn out, all understandable to Jan. Was not her father one of eight children from a long-established Buckinghamshire family? Among his surviving brothers and sisters was not one a local Aylesbury solicitor, another a local architect, another a managing director of a county publishing company? Was not Stanley Wilkins himself a retired colonial civil servant who had been in charge of the administration of the Palestine railway system before sections of it had been blown up by the Irgun Zvai? And would not Jan be considered to be an outsider, a young man from somewhere on the European mainland about to marry an only daughter?

The wedding could be arranged to take place only days before Jan was due to leave for Germany. On an impulse, he persuaded Hilary to honeymoon before the due day. The pair departed for the Isle of Skye, where they stayed in a crofter's cottage and walked on the Cuillins in the rain. On some mornings, when the rainfall was less intense, the crofter would greet them with, "Not a bad day!", but they were content. The cottage was snug.

The wedding was held in the hamlet church close to Ilona's cottage. She, of course, played the organ. Mason Ballard was the best man. There was a reception in Aylesbury's largest hotel, where the extensive Wilkins family was predominant. Two days later, Jan recrossed the English Channel on peacetime military service.

The former immigrant was back on the European mainland, in the country of the former would-be conquerors. Rheindahlen was bristling with signs of a foreign army, now no longer post-war forces of occupation, but professed friendly partners in a struggle against communism. The Commanding Officer of the 42nd Squadron, George Templar, was welcoming, as was his wife, Jean, who enthused, "Your wife will soon be over to join you. When she comes over on her vacations, she will love Friday evenings in the officers' mess. Such fun! They're central in all our postings."

Jan's introduction to his platoon was made on the first

day of his arrival on the barrack square. He ruefully examined the situation. He might be wearing a peaked cap and have an epaulette on his shoulder, but he was the least experienced member of this team of fifteen full-time servicemen which included a sergeant, a corporal, a lance-corporal and twelve other soldiers, most of whom would have served in 'theatres of war'. But this, he told himself, was the system. He knew that he would be helped to learn.

In the following weeks and months, the platoon was often away from its Rheinland headquarters. Support was always taken: the one-ton truck, the two champs, the surveying equipment, the tents, cookers and general provisions. Each day, new localities would be photographed, measurements made, levels checked, star shots and moon shots coordinated, maps revised. The team members' working routines became second nature to them as they travelled the country, always preferring to be on the move rather than at base with its parades and inspections. Over a year and a half, the young officer and his team grew to know each other closely. All shared respect for each other and for the responsibilities which the army had allocated to each one.

A month before Jan was due to be 'demobbed', he was summoned to the headquarters office. George Templar and another senior officer asked him to sit down.

His commanding officer began in personal terms: "Jan, no more mapping for your last weeks. We want you to take the platoon southwards, to the Black Forest. There, you will rendezvous with an American army group with whom you will liaise. The American army over here has no surveyor support, so your team will carry out whatever the Americans want. The platoon will still need to be fully equipped. Your movement orders are in this envelope. Good luck. See you in a month."

The meeting was over.

A week later, on a prescribed day and place, the English platoon arrived to pitch camp in a remote clearing at the end of a lane in the eastern Black Forest, some distance from any settlement. A few hours later, at a set time, three jeeps rolled into the clearing.

A heavily built, loosely dressed lieutenant colonel, with a holstered pistol slung low over one hip, jumped from the first jeep with a, "Hi, you lot, who's the boss here?"

Jan came over to salute.

The American waved a return salute into the trees and shook hands. He introduced himself: "I'm Hank Dorfenstein," he said. "From German immigrants to the States. Funny, isn't it? These guys," he waved his hands towards his nine men, "will all become familiar to you as we work together. In the meantime, we're hungry. We see that you've started a fire. Can we all eat first? We can contribute our US-standard military rations; they don't taste bad, even from tins. Tell us what you think…"

After the meal, the English conceded that American tinned food was the best. Then, under the stars, plans were made.

The lieutenant colonel did the talking: "In this Cold War, our government thinks we have to be prepared for anything. Including a nuke exchange. Now, Russia could believe that our weaponry in the US of A is far enough away from Moscow to give the Soviets the chance of a first-strike advantage. But if they knew that we could return a near-simultaneous strike from here in mainland Europe, then there's hope of stalemate, no attacks, both sides too scared of 'mutual self-destruction'." He paused. "We want you British to help us. We have atomic missiles mounted on trailers. We need to be able to place the missiles directly on top of built trigonometrical points, with each point's location calculated to within six decimal places here on the earth's surface. That's where you come in. We want you to set up a number of such trig points, each with its own particular known coordinates, on a range of Black Forest hills. From any one location we will be able, if necessary, to fire north-east at Moscow." He paused again. He was looking at Jan, who was thinking, *Is this what I was made for?*

"Agreed."

A wide arc of six hills was chosen. On the crown of each hill, the surveyors set up a trig point: a single concrete pillar topped with an inset lead cross. On clear nights, theodolites were placed over each cross, from which readings of known star positions were taken. The resultant readings were then extrapolated to find the exact location of each cross, outcomes which were then passed on to the Americans.

Within two weeks, the surveyors' tasks were complete.

"We're grateful to you Brits," said Hank. "We'll all be safe now."

Jan was less certain.

Goodbyes were said. Cross-Atlantic invitations were extended. The Americans drove away. The British contingent headed home to Rheindahlen.

Jan completed his Black Forest report some days before he was due to be demobilised. There followed a last party with his platoon, a last round of beers in the officers' mess, last hugs and good wishes from the Templars. With just seventy-two hours of Jan's military service remaining, George Templar ordered him to visit Berlin. There, subject to remaining in uniform, he was to join several escorted walking tours of the Eastern Sector.

"Be useful," George said. "See what's going on."

The official planned and guided Eastern Sector routes passed streets and buildings carefully retained to show their wartime ruined state. Stops were arranged before stone memorials erected to commemorate the victorious Russian wartime campaigns, the victorious fallen Russians. Each memorial was illuminated by flaming torches while troops, Russian and East German, stood stoically on guard.

At the end of the third day, Jan flew back to Rheindahlen and onward to England. He was a civilian again. A full life lay ahead.

PART TWO

2019

•

1

Spring 2019

"YOU'LL ALWAYS BE a bloody foreigner."

Jan was accustomed to his friend's confrontational remarks. Peter liked to be challenging; this was how he played chess: attack, attack, ever attack, right from the start of the game.

"Look," Jan said. "I've been in this country for some eighty years, ever since I arrived as a six-year-old. You have been alive here for only seventy years."

Peter quipped back: "But that's not the same. You may have learnt to play cricket and rugby, you may have been commissioned in our army. You may have married an English girl and fathered English-born children, but you'll always have come from somewhere else, so will always be an outsider, still belonging elsewhere."

Peter was continuing to enjoy himself: "And look at what you've really done for this country: you've taken a home-bred Englishman's or Englishwoman's job. Someone of English birth could have been head of a university department instead of you."

Jan stayed patient. "Oh, come on! What do you mean by 'our army'? And what do you mean by 'truly English'? Haven't we all come from Neanderthal or African ancestors?"

Both men were drinking morning coffee at their usual downtown meeting place. Their verbal exchanges were cut short by the arrival of two other academic colleagues, both also retired. All four former professors met at monthly intervals so that they might stay in touch with each other. At such meetings, they had agreed to debate mutually chosen subjects of interest, maybe enlightened by the combined knowledge of Jan (architecture), of Peter (sociology), of Gordon (history) and of Leonard (medicine).

"Not that our talks will be worthwhile," Peter had muttered. "I don't know why we even bother. Not one of us, possibly with the exception of Jan, is in the least willing to hear what the others have to say. Each of us is so self-engrossed, is such a self-publicist, is so full of his own research underway, of that book just published or in preparation, of the lectures he is still giving, here or on well-paid cruises. We pepper each of our sentences with first person singulars, all 'me' and 'my' and 'I'. Why can't we hold back to appreciate each other? The only matter we agree about is that the university is no longer as good as it was in our day."

That morning's meeting was intended to explore the recent Brexit vote.

Peter was quick to start: "Obvious. Quite obvious. Just a complete disaster. Badly managed. Our self-serving political leaders had, and still have, no calibre. Just a useless, dithering, vacuous bunch who take short-term decisions and even get those completely wrong. I loathe them."

"Hold on," Jan cautioned. "Could we just keep our discussions balanced? Could we calmly consider why there were not more voters like us, who wanted to stay in a Europe united at last after generations of inbred wars and slaughter? We were happy at last to remain as equals alongside even our old wartime enemies, the Germans, who had looked Nazism in the face and had worked hard over many years to change themselves, to become liberal, democratic, thoughtful partners of other European nations."

Peter wouldn't be swayed. "But more than half the UK voters wanted to leave a country still riddled by deep-seated English notions about class and privilege which successive governments haven't had the balls to adjust, let alone eradicate. So, the 'us' and the 'them' divisions continued. We were the 'us' lot, weren't we? We were the smug ones who wanted to stay, who thought ourselves to be as much European as British. We who live in university locations, Bristol, Brighton, London, Cambridge, Edinburgh, our children going to top universities where they perpetuated their privileged dreams of living and working across Europe and the world. We who wanted that world to keep on arriving here too, for world trade to keep on openly flowing, even as we accepted unequal wealth distributions, nationally or worldwide, in which digital companies can become richer than individual countries in what's supposed to be a world order of ideal economic liberalism but which doesn't work anymore, and no one has the vision to replace it." He barely paused. "As for 'them', who were they? Who are they now? They're mostly at the bottom of the pile. They remain undereducated, too many still unable to properly speak their own language, no idea of their own grammar, not enough words at their own disposal, reduced to substituting missing vocabulary with expletives, fuckin' this and fuckin' that. Even their supply of swear words is limited. They are fed rubbish TV programmes, with so-called celebrities cavorting in jungles. If we need statistics to support such a notion of social inequality, we find that it's the 'them's who eat the most junk food, who become the most diabetes-ridden members of society, who have the largest proportion of teenage pregnancies of any European country, with sixteen- to nineteen-year-olds the poorest educated among the world's wealthier countries."

Peter tried to round off: "They had so many reasons to be angry. No one had listened to them, their needs hadn't been addressed, they'd been left behind by a governing class which had been providing them with inadequate education, inadequate health and social care, inadequate housing, reduced job opportunities, reduced incomes. The world's sixth wealthiest country? Not for them. Some were among the homeless sheltering in shop doorways. Some were visiting the food banks located in most towns. No wonder they mistakenly blamed their situation on immigrants. They had to hit back by voting in anger and desperation to leave Europe." He hesitated. "Then, of course, they were joined by an unlikely fellow group of voters, a rump of the elderly 'us' lot, who falsely hoped that by leaving Europe we would return to past UK glory days when we had an empire supported by thriving industries and a big navy. What rubbish dreams."

He ended as he had begun… by grumbling. "No leadership to sort it. Out we came. Maybe our traditional religious leaders could have helped to steer us, but they too have lost moral authority. Their congregations dwindle. Just look at the people on *Songs of Praise*. Mostly a grey- and white-haired lot. What happens when they all die off?"

Jan and Leonard hesitated, allowing Gordon to take over: "You may well be right. But history will make Brexit seem like a fly on the wall if we can't resolve world solutions within a global context. Climate change hovers over us. Our greed leads to systems of overproduction which pollute and ravage and reduce the earth's resources, all in turn annihilating our wildlife, unleashing growing plagues and pestilences which will increasingly attack us all. Our planet is overpopulated. We are already at eight billion plus and populations not only continue to increase but are also on the move. Africa migrates across the Med and into Europe. They're coming our way and we can't cope with them. Everywhere, political instability grows. Parts of what we like to think of as our 'free world' become disenchanted, with growing followers of authoritarian demagogues who offer unattainable dreams. Antagonisms increase between nations: we have the US versus China, North versus South Korea, Russia versus the Crimea, India versus Pakistan, Arab state versus Arab state, Israel versus the Arab states combined. Simultaneously, major faith traditions smoulder into antagonisms between fanatics on each side, with extreme Muslins becoming jihadists, with extreme white nationalists becoming neo-fascists. A future war becomes possible between the two great world religions, Muslim versus Judo-Christian. Can our liberal cultures prevent such a collision? Then there's the overall nuclear clock, presently set at two minutes to midnight, the closest it's been since 1953 at the height of the Cold War. Now we have far stronger nuclear, and indeed biological, weapons of destruction, with possible calculating nutters preparing ways to deliver them. Deaths after any major war would be in the hundreds of millions, maybe in billions."

It was Leonard's chance not to be outdone: "Yes, yes, all also possibly true. But we could be finished off even earlier. We are promised viruses and pandemics which could knock us out even in the near future. They might come accidentally or with the evil intentions of groups or nations, who may even now be concocting plagues for future delivery. Surveying disasters might even become our norm. Stephen Hawkins reckoned that the chances of total earth collapse would rise to a near certainty in the next one to ten thousand years. But perhaps we shouldn't worry… our great-grandchildren may never even become aware of the challenges which we are discussing. Long before the world is on its way out, their genes will have been tampered with, their intelligence modified. They'll be part human, part robotic, races of cyborgs conditioned to be content with whatever context they inhabit."

Peter would again not be left out. He just had to crash back: "Who's worrying? Not me! No one needs to bother meddling with me. I'm almost finished now. Age has already done that. Shakespeare was right. Everything goes: your bones, your muscles, your hearing, your sight, your sense of taste and smell, your thoughts, your memory and ultimately, your personality, your very self. Why should we not be angry? For a while longer, I can still see the world with a young man's outlook. On a bus, I can look with appreciation at a beautiful girl with long legs, but she no longer responds… that is unless she is offering me a seat or her mother calls me 'dearie'…"

He kept going: "Meanwhile, we oldies get more lonely. In the last ten years or more we've all seen the health of most of our friends go downhill, starting to be attacked by one cancer or another, or by heart disease, or motor neurone disease, or multiple sclerosis or whatever, and while they're trying to hold out against these malignant onslaughts, their brains also become targets; they suffer the slow, relentless, withering of their mental facilities while their dear ones are weighed down by hopeless efforts to stave off this terror. Some of our friends have, of course, been the lucky ones… I've recently, probably like you all, attended rounds of funerals. I have at times silently hoped that I would join the dead, blissfully released by a quick heart attack, ideally having occurred in flagrante delicto."

He peered at the others. "And here, I look at you three. How can you be complacent when your time is running out? Aren't you just so pessimistic that, as we become weaker, beset by illness, no longer seriously listened to, no longer able to battle with full energy for the right causes, the world becomes alien to us? Are you not in despair because you will never do so many of the things that you were put on this earth to do? I shudder when I look at my bookshelves and see that there are still books to be read or reread and I know that I will never read them. I despair that there are women that I want to love but now never will. That's terrible, don't you think?"

Peter at last knew when to stop. He turned to look away from the others, muttering to himself for a few more moments before finally becoming silent.

Jan tried to change the mood. "We also know that there's still so much beauty in the world, so much creativity, all that youth with optimism, with that fervour to change the world, to do better. Tell you what, why don't we also try to do something different together? Maybe go on a trip together?"

Peter, unusually, did not disagree. "Why not? Where might you propose we go?"

"Come with Charlotte and me to Karlovy Vary."

"Where the hell's that?"

"Karlovy Vary is a spa town in the middle of Europe, in former Bohemia. It's where this 'bloody foreigner' whom you like to tease was born. An international film festival is held there each year in early July. We might all have fun! And we could all take the waters! Why don't we all ask our partners if they would like to come with us?"

Home discussions were held and decisions made. Leonard and his wife Hester were unable to change earlier plans. Gordon and his wife Bridget, one of his history degree students whom he had married soon after she had gained her qualifications, reluctantly excused themselves.

Jan's second wife, Charlotte, an actress, keenly looked forward to the film festival.

"I've researched it," she said. "Apparently Julianne Moore will be there!"

Peter's most recent partner was an artist, Louise, some thirty years younger than him. She, also, was full of enthusiasm: "I'm going to bring at least two sketchbooks."

2

IN LATE JUNE, their train from London via Brussels slid into Prague's main line station.

"It's Hlavní nádraží now," Jan said. "Long gone are the days when it was Wilsonova station, Czech homage to president Woodrow Wilson and his support for the 1918 setting-up of our new nation."

The building seemed unchanged from the image in Jan's head, though life on the arrival platform was certainly different from the scenes of 1938. Now, a group of English revellers had already begun to celebrate the start of their midweek-long stag party. Many were clutching beer cans. There was confusion. In the middle of much shouting and pushing, one reveller was violently sick. Another slid on the vomit and fell. Jan thought, *Welcome back. At least, today, people are free to spew.*

All four travellers took a taxi. There was no time to observe the station's main Art Nouveau frontage because the driver was in a hurry, remaining unsmiling and uncommunicative during the short journey to their hotel in Wenceslas Square.

On arrival, he did not return their *dekujis* and *na shledanous*. Charlotte thought that he must be worried. Before they walked into the hotel lobby, Jan pointed to the features of the square, the museum at the top of the slope, Wenceslas on his horse, the cafés.

"There are more adverts than I can remember," he said. "And more traffic and noise and agitation. Except, look over there, today's chess players are still peaceful and calm; they could be the children and grandchildren of the men whose games I used to watch."

The hotel was one of those big, impersonal places geared to a thriving international tourist market. The narrow red carpet on long upper-floor corridors may have been intended to bring joy to tourist's hearts. Instead, each red line, stretching to a dim infinity, made Louise slightly anxious.

"They point to distant corners which change directions into the unknown…"

The four quickened their steps to reach the havens of their rooms. They slept late. The first-floor breakfast space was crowded. A large waitress dressed in black swept them to a table which had just been vacated and so had not yet been cleared. Around the room, some ten such women, all similarly large and uniformed in black, were serving the tourists. The waitresses appeared to have been trained within the bounds of a peculiar etiquette of hospitality which disallowed any smiling or gestures of helpfulness towards guests. Instead, an air of grim service appeared to prevail, with language barriers maintained and even fortified.

"What's all this about?" Charlotte asked Jan, remembering

the taxi driver. "We're not in an occupied country anymore, surely?"

He tried to make some sense of it for her. "For so long the Czechs and Slovaks have been dominated by others; for four centuries they were part of the old Austro-Hungarian Habsburg Empire, ruled from Vienna. My country was the new Czechoslovakia, only formed in 1918 under its philosopher president Masaryk, only to last twenty years in charge of its own destiny until 1938, when the Germans invaded and remained in power till 1945. Then came more control, this time by the Russians and the eastern block, lasting till the 'Velvet Revolution' of 1989, since when self-rule has emerged. Today the Czechs can all hold up their heads as a self-directed nation. But some still seem to retain a brooding, pessimistic outlook, only too ready to become petty officials, getting their own back on the world for past injustices. Our taxi driver, these waitresses, older clerks in ticket offices, all conform to a picture of retaliation, though hopefully a new generation is breaking the habit."

"Thanks for that," she said. "When the coffee arrives, why don't we just give our waitress some nice smiles?"

They stayed only for a few days, the four walking together everywhere. Jan was surprised by the infiltration of so many souvenir shops and fast-food joints. "Probably no different from anywhere in the world right now?"

The others nodded. They were nevertheless enjoying the permanent beauty of Prague.

Jan showed them places which had marked his time in the city: the arcades of the old town, the banks of the Vltava, the bridges, the nursery school altered and extended but still in its own courtyard. They sat in a Wenceslas Square café and watched a game of chess from the beginning to the end. Even Peter remained quiet.

On the second day, they began walking on Hradčany's castle hillside. From a café terrace, with its vine tendril-covered walls, they looked down over the river and the city.

"What a wedding cake," Peter said. "Must still be the most beautiful city in Europe. How come the Germans didn't smash it?"

"We let them come in without resisting," Jan replied. "Our caretaker President's orders!"

"I notice you still say 'we' and 'our'!"

"I can't help it, can I?"

They moved on to visit the Strahov monastery, silenced into awe by its Baroque library, fascinated by its seventeenth-century collection of astronomical globes.

"Yes, I spun that big one when I was a child," Jan confessed.

In the late afternoon, Jan showed them a Frank Gehry building close to the Vltava's south-eastern bank. "Those two forms sloping into each other, the locals call them Fred and Ginger, a reminder of Astaire and Rogers dancing together. Peter, you'll talk of American culture taking over. Maybe you should wait till we reach the film festival."

3

THE EVENING TRAIN journey from Prague to Karlovy Vary took some three hours, a route not officially recommended by the Czech tourist office, which advised shorter bus travel instead.

"Let's go by rail anyway," Jan had said. "I want to move backwards on my life's track."

They reached Karlovy Vary's railway station on the evening of 27th June. Posters along the arrival platform announced the start next day of the 54th International Film Festival.

"Many will be staying at the Grand Hotel Pupp," Jan told them. "As we will, though we can't afford it." He turned to Charlotte. "Maybe you'll be spotted by a famous Eastern European director and be given a contract! You'll be more beautiful than any of the film stars."

Charlotte rolled her actress's eyes at the heavens in feigned exasperation at his boyish humour, which she rather enjoyed.

Meanwhile, he was pulling them forwards and out of

the building. "Come on, hurry up; there may be surprises for us."

The street lamps had been switched on and looked festive.

"Over there is the Ohře-Tepla river junction. Looks as if they've built a new, wider footbridge over the Ohře; we were so nearly blown up on the old, narrow one. And yes, look, there are our surprises: special forms of transport to the hotel; they've been waiting for us since the thirties."

Alongside an avenue of trees stretched a row of horse-drawn carriages, each item of carriage work gleaming in the reflected light of each individual coach lamp, the coachmen patient, their groomed steeds impatient, shaking their harnesses, stamping their hooves.

"Let's all jump in."

The four visitors and their cases filled the leading carriage, which was immediately drawn southwards at a brisk trot. In the gathering dusk, the transition between new town and old town was blurred.

"I'll explain it all to you tomorrow," Jan said. "All I know or can remember, that is."

They were content anyway, immersed in the newness of the trip, swaying with the swaying of the horse. Within minutes, their route began to narrow between steep hillsides and denser, older buildings which squeezed out the remaining daylight. Now the old town sparkled artificially as the carriage moved quickly forwards in its dreamlike setting towards the Hotel Pupp. With a flourish, their coachman swung his steed on an arc into a wide courtyard, even more brightly illuminated than the surrounding town.

Here, there was much activity, many visitors and many greetings. Under a canopy of flags, the unloading of luggage was taking place from large cars, as well as from carriages similar to their own, the horses still restless after their short journey. Several young women were laughing with their coachmen.

"Starlets, your rivals," Jan teased Charlotte.

"In your dreams," she said. "Because I'd be playing their mother."

Nearby, some photographers were taking flash pictures of a new group of evidently important arrivals, the men nonchalant, the women throwing their heads back to show better necklines or to reveal more bosom. At that moment, a very shiny airport taxi arrived. An elegantly dressed woman stepped out, at once to be surrounded by hotel staff.

"Yes, as I thought, that's Julianne Moore," Charlotte pointed out. "Wow! I wonder what film she'll be in, or maybe she's just a visitor."

They had planned the whole trip on a modest budget. After registering, they made their way to two rooms in an annexe wing facing a rear courtyard.

"Lovely," Charlotte said. "Lots of room to move about. These old buildings are so spacious." She flung her arms around Jan's neck and giggled. "Who's hungry?" she asked. "Can we go and eat?"

They strolled back through the hotel's foyers and lounges, past a large restaurant set within neoclassical splendour, alongside a bar from the mid-European nineteenth century, then past a second bar out of London's 1920s, from which drifted the syncopations of live Harlem jazz.

"My god, what a mix," Peter said. "It's all here: dream spaces filling up with dreamers and dream makers even before the films begin."

They walked out into the front courtyard again, avoiding another group of posing celebrities. Beyond the hotel frontage, they found a small restaurant and settled down to their meal.

"Tomorrow, will we search for your childhood home?" Louise asked.

"Maybe not. Maybe on our last day, before we leave. We can first take in several days of cinema."

Louise asked if, after all this time, he might be scared to search.

"Sure, a bit," Jan said.

Next morning, they ate breakfast in the main restaurant. Menus indicated sumptuous choices of food and drink as befitted one of Europe's former grand hotels. Many of the tables were already occupied.

"Listen to that babble of tongues," Peter said. The hum of conversation included languages from around the world, with predominant Russian and Slavonic accents mingling with voices from central Europe, Scandinavia, Greece, the Middle East and America. Visitors and performers had risen early to make sure they missed none of the festival's first-day events. In a far corner sat the starlets who had been such conspicuous arrivals on the previous evening. Would they feature in one of the week's films or were they here just hoping for future fame?

The coffee was good. They took in views of columns and cornices, of ornate plaster ceilings and glistening chandeliers, of gleaming silverware and hovering ready-to-please waiters with deferential smiles.

"Unlike those aggressive women in Prague," Peter said. "Except they could have similar feelings, but here, more money is making them smile. Money, still money, always the same driver in the past and present, sod it. In the thirties, spread by industrialists and by all that European and Russian aristocracy. Now, generated by film stars and celebrities, the new aristocracy. We're just out of place."

Charlotte and Louise smiled. Not inclined to be philosophical, they and Jan continued instead to enjoy their breakfasts.

While her friends continued to contemplate the surrounding scene, Charlotte went to pick up information and leaflets from the festival shop located within the hotel's main entrance hall. She returned excited. She was such a film fan.

"Quite a choice," she said. "Independent films from all over the world. There's a focus on European production, with a further section called 'East of the West' to cover Russia, the Ukraine, Estonia and Latvia. There are apparently over two hundred feature-length films, as well as a large documentary section. And all these choices are showing over just five days of the festival. We could see a lot within each day and evening. It's all starting at ten this morning across the river and up at the Hotel Thermal's Grand Hall. It seems that discussions between director and audience take place after each showing, isn't that marvellous? And there'll also be a grand jury making awards at the end."

They moved out into the hotel courtyard before crossing the Tepla by the nearest footbridge and walking on to reach the Grand Hall. Large crowds had already gathered between the Hall and the riverside. All ages were represented. Clapping rippled and cameras flashed as a woman in a bright yellow billowing dress stepped onto the entrance podium. Julianne Moore, smiling broadly and clutching a trophy, spoke briefly in English to accept her 2019 Festival Award for 'outstanding contribution to world cinema'. Then, the festival was formally opened.

Photographers continued to hover. Shouts arose when a long Škoda drew up to deposit two smiling and waving people by the Hall's wide entrance steps.

"Must be important, maybe the stars of the film, do you know them?" people asked.

"No," others replied. "But both are so young, so beautiful. And wouldn't you just die for those dresses?"

Two and a half hours later, the thousand-strong audience emerged into sunlight. Few people were talking. During the film, the crowded auditorium had been subdued, while the follow-up discussion with the film's director had become intense and argumentative.

"Why are you preaching at us?" a man had shouted. "Why all these politics? Why can't you give us a bit more escapism; isn't that what cinema is for? You gave us doom and gloom. No enjoyment. The world needs to enjoy, doesn't it?"

The director had stood her ground. Her Czech film, called *Let There Be Light*, had shown a Slovak village preparing for Christmas. The main character, forty-year-old Milan, had returned from working in Germany to be at home with his family. He found that his son had become a member of a fascist paramilitary youth organisation.

"Escapism doesn't help today's world," the director had countered. "The truth, as we see it, is far more essential. I wanted to say that compassion must battle xenophobia. I wanted to hold up a mirror to ourselves."

The audience cheered.

In the sunshine, the two visiting couples stood quietly. Looking up to the hillsides surrounding the town roofs, they again became acclimatised to their surroundings.

"That was good," Peter unusually acknowledged. "The whole thing did feel like the truth, just real lives which one can continue to think about. We try to escape into cinema, but some films won't let us escape. They're saying, *Look, this is how it is, this is how you are.*"

Now, the audience was moving away, so many from the younger generation, all in T-shirts, shorts and sandals. The promenades on each side of the Tepla were again filling up.

Peter remained a questioner. "Films thoughtful, yes, but young spectators maybe not for long? Do they lack attention span? Instead of talking to each other, they are already click-clacking into their mobile phones, their digital world immediately following their film world. OK, it's good that they can connect at speed to others across the globe with their Facebooks, their WhatsApps and their Instagrams linking them to other young, like-minded billions. And OK, it's good that they have their Google opportunities to get information, again at speed, on almost any subject. But there's the downside. Their personal privacy, and ours, is being bartered away, with Facebook and Google's computerised information on us already being used by others for their own ends."

Louise felt that she could intrude. "Look, we are hungry. Why don't we have some lunch?"

They crossed a footbridge to sit on a café terrace on Stará Louka, west of the river. They ate sandwiches and drank juice while they watched the passers-by.

Peter continued to be commentator. "Look at those older, smarter strollers carrying their shopping bags. They're still the international tourist set, helping brand-name shops to do great business. Look how they pour into Versace or into that Moser glass showroom to buy and buy through the afternoon. They're just lounging and idling, looking and being looked at, hoping that three weeks of sanatorium regimes of healthy eating, pummelling and creaming will counteract their annual excessive appetites. Unlike the youngsters we saw this morning, this lot looks as if they do want to escape; they don't want to notice the poor in their dream world. But then, I suppose that escapism was always the nature of this place?"

Jan chose not to take up his friend's challenge.

Fortunately, Louise stayed cheerful. "Why don't we join the throng? Let's stroll along the Thermal Colonnade. We can sip the waters and, if we don't like the taste, we can drown it with a glass of Becherovka, apparently digestive tonic made from herbs. And we can add some of the local 'oblaten' hazelnut wafers."

Charlotte and Jan quickly agreed. They began walking. From a kiosk, each hired one of the town's famous porcelain beakers, filling this with waters which gushed and steamed from parallel rows of spouts regularly located between lines of columns. They drank.

Charlotte was the first to splutter. "Oh dear. How can people drink this stuff? Now I can understand why the Lonely Planet Guide called it 'sulphurous gunk'! Look at what it's doing to the ends of each spout outlet; is that what our insides will look like?"

Jan still held mild allegiance to the ritual. "Sweetheart, that's what one of my mother's friends used to say, but I have to tell you that people have been drinking 'this stuff' for six hundred years and you can see that visitors still keep coming back."

In the late afternoon, they returned to the hotel. Charlotte wanted to change because Jan had volunteered an evening outing to a small restaurant in the town. The Pupp's dinner menu was too expensive for them and 'too lavish, anyway', Charlotte and Louise had agreed. At the festival desk, a group of guests surrounded the information board. Charlotte walked over eagerly, then returned. "They've confirmed the showing of a Bulgarian film called *The Father*. We can see it at seven o'clock back at the Hotel Thermal. Let's not eat till afterwards. Louise and I aren't hungry yet, anyway."

Both women changed their outfits.

"Don't they look stunning?" Jan asked Peter, who merely shrugged his shoulders.

The vast auditorium at the Hotel Thermal was packed with the evening's visitors, their concentration immediately centred on the opening images. The Father was *Vasil*, a widowed artist trying to hold himself together after losing his wife. She had apparently told a neighbour that she had to speak to Vasil about something of great importance, but she died before doing so. Vasil believes that his wife is trying to use his phone in efforts to reach him from beyond the grave. He asks a psychic to help him make contact. Simultaneously, Vasil's son tries to dissuade him, afraid that his father is becoming demented. The two disagree. Other members of their family intervene. Outcomes are both comical and absurd. What will happen?

In the subsequent open discussion, the film's two Bulgarian directors explained that they wanted to highlight poor communication between parents, their children and often close families.

"Communication with the past, the present and the future… all fails… as does our own communication with ourselves and our own feelings."

At dinner that night, Peter was once again uncritical. "More realistic lives… how do these central and eastern European filmmakers do it? Perhaps because their own lives have been so tough?"

Both couples spent the following two afternoons and evenings viewing more films. Themes of real life continued to spread through the showings, whether in major feature films or in documentaries. Among Jan and Charlotte's choices was *Patrick*, billed as a tragicomedy. Young Patrick is in charge of maintenance work at a nudist campsite owned by his father. He keeps the maintenance workshop well-ordered, but when he loses his favourite hammer, a chain of events is set off which show that orderliness and openness, whether in a workshop or a nudist camp or elsewhere, still leaves much which remains hidden.

In discussion time following the screening, the film's

Belgian director was asked why he and the scriptwriters had chosen this very particular setting.

He replied, "In life, certainty can never be guaranteed. We can never be sure how humour, or even grief will affect us. We all seek dignity… even if we don't wear trousers!"

Peter and Louise had chosen to watch documentary films, Peter's preference to which Louise had readily agreed. They relayed their viewing experiences back to Jan and Charlotte. Peter was spokesperson: "We went to a showing which was a selection of movies shot between 1989 and 1992, all commemorating the thirtieth anniversary of the six-week Velvet Revolution. What a time that must have been, that amazing bloodless overthrow of a Communist regime. So much Czech hope followed, so much artistic freedom of the kind we are seeing this week."

Jan, for once, did the countering: "Unless totalitarianism comes back…"

Louise took over from Peter. "We also went to a different showing. We saw eleven remastered films made by the famous Egyptian director and producer Youssef Chahine, born 1926, died 2008. Marvellous, iconic films. Three had English subtitles but these were hardly needed. All were about the lives of poor people living in city or countryside. Scenarios clearly attacked authority and unjust oppression. Why hasn't Chahine been more celebrated in England? Full marks again to this festival."

Morning excursions were taken in the town or on the surrounding pine-covered hillsides. Peter, Louise and Charlotte readily accepted Jan as their guide. He took them to the familiar places of his childhood, often expressing surprise at how little had changed. Their otherwise brisk walks were punctuated and slowed down whenever they waited for Louise to complete another of her sketches. They were jointly proud of her sketchbooks.

"So much better than our photos! She captures more than we can see!"

Their longest wait was when Jan took them further along the Tepla's east bank to the church of St Mary Magdalene. "Dientzenhofer's Baroque masterpiece of the 1730s," Louise enthused as she made several fast drawings of the exterior and interior. She would have stayed even longer had she dared.

Close by was the Vridlo thermal spring rotunda, its glass-covered walls clouded in steam, with figures inside just moving shadows.

"Seventy-three degrees of centigrade heat," Jan said. "The Vridlo must have been jetting up its treasure in twelve-metre-high thrusts, even during the moments when my mother and I and those crowds were running by, and we didn't even notice. It'll be pushing some eleven thousand gallons of water into the air every hour for hundreds more years after we've gone."

Then, Jan took them past the Art Nouveau flats on Vridelni Street and onwards north-west to the Mill Colonnade. "That's where my friends and I played each week while our mothers had coffee together. And over there, at Mülbrun Street, is where my parents' dental surgery was located. I always had to pretend to be the perfect child patient, so when other children came for real treatment, they could see that there was no need to cry."

When they reached the sixteen-storey Hotel Thermal, Jan became more reflective. "Here we are again, our festival venue, the flags decking out that marvellous circular brut concrete plinth which heralds the auditorium for twelve hundred people. This area used to be a traditional townscape when I was a boy. Now, the Lonely Planet describes the whole thing as a scab, but I think the building is great, even heroic, seventies symbolism for all the town's citizens and visitors. For a forty-year period, between 1948 and 1989, the country's imposed Communist regime, backed by Russia, remodelled the cultural and social life of Karlovy Vary. Spa facilities were nationalised, with treatments becoming free to Czechs. Our hotel Pupp became 'Grandhotel Moskva'. The Műhlbrunnen Kolonnade was alternatively called 'Gagarin Kolonnade' or 'Czechoslovak-Soviet Friendship Kolonnade'. The eastern hillside funicular railway ascended from 'Lenin Square'. They thought that by changing the names of places, they could wipe out the past. After the Velvet Revolution of 1989, the Czechs similarly thought they could then wipe out forty-four years of Communism by changing all the names back to their original state, so Moskva again became Pupp, et cetera, et cetera."

A last stop on one of Jan's tours took them back to the Hotel Pupp, besides which the town's second funicular was still in operation. They bought some bread, cheese, fruit and wine in a nearby shop, queued for one-way tickets and were soon pulled up into the hills. The surrounding woods were greener than Jan ever could recall. Sunlight glinted on silver birch among the pine trees. Within minutes, they arrived at the Diana Tower station. On a small terrace, groups of mothers talked while their children played nearby.

"Still the same as it ever was on my mother's Thursday outings." Jan was laughing. "Look at the steps winding upwards. A hundred and fifty of them. It took me only four minutes to get to the top, but alas I won't run today. Would any of you like to try?"

There were no volunteers for a speedy ascent, though Louise, as the youngest, slowly climbed all the way until she waved down to them from the tower's lookout platform.

"I'm a huntress," she called. "And I'm coming to get you."

They laughed. After Louise had returned to them, Jan seemed restless.

"I can't leave without trying again. Who will time me?"

"Don't be silly!" Charlotte reacted immediately. "You are aged nearer ninety than eighty. Please don't be so silly."

Louise and Peter backed her. "No time for heroism, old pal," Peter said.

"All right then, I'll go up slowly. Who will time me?"

They gave in.

"Slowly then," Peter said. "For God's sake, slowly."

They watched him disappear.

They waited silently. Fifteen minutes later, Jan's head appeared over the lookout railing above. Charlotte was anxious. Louise held her arm.

Peter said: "I'll go up to help him down."

They found a resting place and ate and drank. No further mention was made of the Diana Tower.

"Look over there." Jan pointed. "High upon the eastern slope is another big sanatorium hotel, the Imperial. My home is also up there. Tomorrow, shall we search for it?"

The plan was agreed. They all chose to traverse diagonal downwards paths to their own hotel in the valley. Jan was only mildly breathless.

It was their last but one morning.

"Today, we'll find your home," Charlotte said.

The sun was already strong as they left the hotel, first following the valley road eastwards out of town. To their right, the pinewood slopes were in dark shadow. As they reached the Japanese Zen Garden at the edge of Poštovní Park, they branched to the left and began to climb the eastern hillside at Imperial Street. The road swung left and right, then left again, past trees and gardens. Jan and Charlotte climbed arm in arm, her head against his shoulder. Peter and Louise followed. Below them, patterns of roofscapes and treescapes became ever clearer.

"Surprise," Jan said. "So little has changed over eighty years."

The hill's incline now started to flatten out. Before the last bend, he tried to picture what they would see and, as they turned into Imperial Street, there it was: a white, four-storey villa with balconies, all with a backdrop of pine trees, a scene which the villa's modernist architect might have sketched in a perspective drawing for his 1920s clients.

They reached a pair of gates which guarded a pathway leading to the villa entrance porch. He was looking for signs of family life. Instead, several T-shirted people, all in vague middle age, were coming out of the front door and heading in the direction of the funicular station. Jan and Charlotte passed them at the gates and walked on to the porch. A blue plastic plaque was badly screwed to the wall under the porch canopy. Rough translation indicated that the villa was now being used as a holiday and recuperation centre for members of a trade union group. The front door was locked.

Through a glass panel, they could make out a hallway with several subsidiary doors, each with a separate lock and push button bell. On a side wall, there was a noticeboard covered with many sheets of paper.

"Rules and regulations?" Jan queried.

"Are you going to try to get in?" she asked.

He thought of their journey across Europe. "No," he said. "No point. I wouldn't want to see how the inside has changed."

They regained their steps to the gates where Peter and Louise were waiting. All four crossed the road towards the downwards slope of the hill and sat on a low wall above the town. Louise made a rapid sketch of the villa. Jan felt momentarily tired; this was both climax and anticlimax. Should they have come?

Charlotte was holding his arm tightly. He wrapped his arm around her, pulling her closer. In silence, they looked down to the valley and out to the hills beyond. After a while, she asked, "Was it always so beautiful?"

He nodded. "Yes, the same Baroque town, the same Bohemian setting. This is how I remember it looked in the old world. How could it have changed so little after war, after incomprehensible evil, death and revolution?"

They were both silent again, he wrinkling his eyes in the sunshine, she being mysterious behind dark glasses. Peter and Louise had walked further ahead to take in other views of the valley.

Somewhere, a dog barked.

Jan said, "OK, so the place was fortunate. The Germans, the Russians, the Americans, none of them bombed it to hell as they did all those other places which then grew new infrastructures and developed new character. But that's not really the question, is it? The question is: no matter whether things look the same or not, are we now in a very different world?"

She asked, "Aren't rates of change so much faster? So many things are new: the internet, mobile phones, stem cells, cloning, that word they keep using, globalisation – all of that?"

He shook his head. "I meant real essentials – what about us, what about people? My parents may have led slower, outwardly more peaceful, comfortable, idyllic lives, but always underneath and around them, everywhere really, in their social circle, their town, country, continent, world, there was also poverty and inequality, seething prejudice, deceit, selfishness, envy, hatred, greed, all those human conditions and emotions which are still with us today, pushing us into cycles of destruction. Although the First and Second World Wars killed millions, other wars in the world since 1945 have never stopped. We should have learnt so many lessons from the past to make our new world different and better, but is that possible if we humans remain unchanged? I can't help thinking of Peter, Gordon, Leonard and myself, all lecturing to each other just before we left England. Our lists of the world's ills were probably accurate... so isn't the new world becoming worse more quickly than the old?"

She squeezed against him. "You don't really believe all that, do you? You, the eternal optimist? Don't you think it's good that we are more open about the wrongs that exist in the world? Is there not more honesty now, more searching for better ways forward? Aren't we helping others more?"

He took off her sunglasses to kiss her. He said, "Welcome to you, the real eternal optimist! You put me to shame."

Sunshine flooded the roadside. Behind them, the villa seemed empty. He didn't want to let her go.

"Whatever happens," he said, "we can cope. We not only have family and friends and good health and material safety and art and travel and scenery, but even those are just bonuses. The main thing is that we have each other."

The last was half statement, half question. She was too cool to answer. He wouldn't have expected her to answer, though she stayed close.

He asked, "Shall we go join Peter and Louise? We could try the funicular; it's still running." Instead, they called to their friends and all four agreed to walk downhill again. At the bend where Imperial Street began to drop southwards, they looked back to the villa just once more. Jan suddenly found himself wondering about Žofie's family. Had she ever been married? Did she have brothers and sisters or perhaps nieces and nephews who would have adopted Pretty and would have taken her for long walks? Why had he not known these things?

They soon again found themselves in the valley. On Půskinovastezka, by a quiet bank of the Tepla, they stopped before a long, white, two-storey building.

"Art Deco, really fine." Jan waved.

"It's an art gallery, oh please, do let's look." Louise was already running towards the entrance. Inside, all was still. They found that the ground and first floors held a permanent collection of twentieth-century Czech art. There were few other visitors. In many rooms, they were alone with paintings and, in each corner, with a solitary elderly man or woman pretending not to keep watch. They walked mainly in silence, following works from the 1900s onwards.

"Czech artists showed unity with the journey of western painting," Jan said. "The same sequence of isms from Impressionism through Fauvism, Expressionism, Cubism, Futurism, et cetera."

Louise was thrilled. "Here's life each time newly reinterpreted."

When they reached canvases painted from 1940 onwards, Peter was quick to speak out. "From here, honest expression becomes dead. Artists either became propagandists for the ruling regime, Nazi or Communist, or disguised their feelings behind geometric or fantastical compositions or still lifes. Even the printed gallery guide to these works remains vague, we get obscurantist text. Just listen to this: '*painting… 1939 to '45… the wartime atmosphere of the period brought new interest in man, the city and civilisation*'. Or how about this: '*painting during the Russian occupation… testimony to the problems experienced in human life*'. Why don't they just say '*the country was occupied, the artists were scared and they either collaborated or camouflaged the meaning in their work*'?"

Jan agreed. "You might notice that even present-day Czechs use the dual word '*so-called*' when they describe something in writing or speech. It's because they instinctively harp back to a time when it was dangerous to express one's own opinion clearly for fear the authorities would think it the wrong opinion. It was dangerous to call a spade '*a spade*'. One had to be cautious, to hold back. Everything became '*so-called*' because then, unknown outsiders could be held responsible for dodgy ideas."

They walked on. The Hotel Pupp was nearby. They were all still thinking about the gallery's paintings as they walked into the hotel courtyard.

Charlotte looked around. "This place is starting to feel like home. But we have to leave tomorrow."

"I'll do a last sketch," Louise said. "Then supper?"

Later, in the local restaurant which they had made their own, they ate hungrily and drank a lot.

It was Louise who began asking questions. "Jan, tell me more about yourself. In the short time that I've been with Peter, he only tells me about himself. That's what he says academics do. Now, here we are in your birthplace, but I don't really know anything about your career. How much time did you spend being an architect? And how much time being an academic?"

Jan was reluctant to open up. "I was an architect for over sixty-five years, a time which coincided with thirty-five years of teaching. Much of the architectural work was normally carried out within a team framework of like-minded colleagues and ranged across many building types. Early on, we designed a railway station near London, very 'brutalist' in nature, with lots of exposed concrete and dark brickwork. So wonderful, we youthfully thought. Nowadays the station is a Grade II listed building. There followed work carried out within the London County Council's housing division, particularly a mega scheme to rehouse thousands of eastenders on a parkland setting by the Thames near Greenwich. We enthused about 'city walls', with tenants living on what we called 'streets in the air'. Beyond the LCC, there then followed administration buildings for public and private clients – we often used new, prefabricated methods of construction or new notions of internal planning, for example, we were responsible for the first office building in England which had an atrium, or we experimented with 'scissors' building sections which eliminated wasteful corridor circulation. Later came a headquarters building for the south of England's largest firm of solicitors, then residential work, ranging widely between unique, one-off private homes to large-scale public housing projects for a southern New Town. Later still came university buildings, sports buildings, a theatre renovation and, most recently, years of urban design work on a large extension to the county town of East Sussex. There we planned a mixed development of homes, health facilities, shopping and leisure facilities, performance venues, public spaces, landscaping and environmental improvements, including flood defences. Over the years, such projects have received awards, local and national, have been published in the architectural press and have been recorded in Pevsner editions."

"Meanwhile, academia?" Louise asked gently.

"That life was often led in parallel with architectural practice. Architects who taught were encouraged by their institutions to 'practice' also. Our students liked to have tutors who could build what they professed. Students would volunteer to work with us during long vacations. Tutors could group together to form partnerships capable of providing work of quality. I began as a part-time tutor in a School of Art, which later became a department in a polytechnic, which later became a university in which I became head of that university's school of architecture, retiring as Professor Emeritus. Over time, I taught and examined in the UK, in Eastern Europe, in Japan and in America, where I tutored semesters at the universities of Arkansas and Yale. My students, well over a thousand in number, now produce work all over the world. Some are even retired or are at the point of retiring…"

Louise's curiosity was not yet satisfied. "And what about family? Peter says that you are a workaholic. Did you have time for family life?"

"I hope so. You would need to have asked the family, my then-wife, who has sadly died, and our three children. My wife and I shared practical responsibilities from the start of our married life, she as mother and social worker, I as father and architect. We both supported the children's school activities; we shared a home life of family meal taking, of outings with friends, of connections with relatives, of family holidays. Perhaps our children's present lives would give you some clue about their childhood, about their parents' support, including mine. Our daughter became a magazine editor, later a photographer and she is now an established artist. Our elder son, a mathematician, became an aid worker and has, with his wife, set up an international charity. Our younger son became a barrister who now works in the Civil Service. He is an accomplished pianist.

There are also five active grandchildren of ages ranging from twelve to twenty-six." Jan paused. "Do you have enough answers?"

Louise nodded, but she wanted a little more. "And was there anyone who influenced you most in your life?"

"My mother, I suppose. She was the heroine. In the privileged and material world of her youth, she had everything. Then, suddenly, nothing. She and my father were uprooted and with a child to protect. Barely settled in a new country, she became a widow. But she made many new friends, found work, set up a new career... made a home in an English thatched cottage in a country village, where she planted a cottage garden in heavy Buckinghamshire clay, where she became the village church organist, pushing the ancient organ's foot bellows every Sunday evensong. She played Beethoven again on a second-hand upright piano for which she had saved; she took up painting and went to painting classes, joined an English literature group and befriended writers at summer university courses and, when she retired at the age of sixty, became a well-known guide at Waddesdon Manor for many further years, an occupation she enjoyed even more because of the top-up lectures she regularly attended at the British Museum."

"Did she marry again?" Louise asked.

"No. She could never sufficiently forget my father. There was a brief moment towards the end of the war when she grew close to a Czech pilot who was flying with the RAF. But, when peace came, he returned home. She remained single, spending her last years in a NALGO (National Association of Local Government Officers) rest home by the sea in Sussex. There she read a lot, joined art classes, tended her own garden and drove a Mini to collect shopping for her less able friends."

It was late. Louise thanked him. Charlotte said that he looked tired.

Jan said, "Maybe it was the fault of those blessed steps in the Diana Tower." They agreed to stop, to go to sleep. They would all meet for brunch on the next day, their last in Karlovy Vary. No further plans were made.

Back in bed, Charlotte turned into Jan's side.

"There was so much about your mother that I never knew. What a marvellous woman she must have been. So brave. Such a fighter. So active. And always spreading friendship."

"Sweetheart, there's something I couldn't bring myself to tell you all. When Ilona was in her mid-eighties in that NALGO home, she began to get the most terrible and continuous spinal pains. Nothing helped her, neither spine injections nor other available pain relief measures. Her nights were unbearable. One morning, when the staff brought in her usual cup of tea, they found her dead in bed. She had tied a plastic bag around her head in the night."

Charlotte started to cry softly.

Jan attempted consolation. "Don't worry too much, sweetheart. That's how it was. Perhaps we central Europeans have always been more prepared to take our lives lightly. Maybe that's the best thing to do when life gets too much? We have heroic precedents: Stefan and Elizabeth Zweig in Brazil in 1942, Arthur and Cynthia Koestler in England in 1983, each a double suicide. Perhaps the lightness just runs in families? Take mine, grandmother, uncle, mother, three in just my lifetime. Perhaps there have been others."

He tried to suck the wetness from her cheeks. Charlotte continued to hug him until they both fell asleep.

4

EVEN NOW, IT still took him a long time to wake up. She would begin to move when he moved, neither one quite knowing whose leg or arm or hand was being disentangled. He tried to open one eye, then closed it again. Beyond his eyelids, a different white room was filling with light. He thought, *No swing here*.

He said, "Our last day. We promised Peter and Louise that we would meet them for brunch, remember?"

She wriggled and said, "Mmm," and buried her head into the void between his ribs and the mattress sheet. There was no hurry.

Later in the morning, the friends again met on their favourite café terrace. All four were unusually quiet. Even Peter was not inclined to start a customary debate. They drank coffee, watching the passers-by.

"Still here." Peter pointed along the line of shops by the riverbank. "Still out here, the health seekers, the pleasure seekers, the rich and indolent. Look how they avoid that old woman over there in that shop doorway. She's not moving, as if she has been there forever. They side-step her, pretending they haven't seen her. She isn't even begging directly. She is just looking at them. Such an angry look. Her lips are opening and closing. The old crone could be cursing them."

Jan and Charlotte stood up. Charlotte said, "That poor woman, we must give her something." She and Jan walked to the doorway. They put notes into an upturned hat by the woman's side before returning to their table.

Peter muttered, "She just kept staring at you. Nothing more. She is so old."

Their coffee was cold. Louise asked, "Any remaining plans, anyone?"

Jan answered with, "How about a swim up on the hilltop open baths? Who wants to come?"

Charlotte was keen. "I'll swim. I look forward to the female changing rooms. It's rumoured that they are full of unusually large Czech and Russian women."

"I feel too lazy," Peter said.

Louise nodded to confirm that she would stay with Peter.

He laughed. "See, my shadow. We can idle all day, then meet you at the station this evening."

Jan was content. He would just be together with Charlotte on a last afternoon in his first homeland. "We are ready and packed anyway. I'll just take a rucksack with us, for towels and stuff."

As they emerged from the comparative quietness and dim light of the tiled changing rooms, they were unprepared for the sudden explosion of noise and of sunlight blazing down on the open pool. They both jumped in, and Jan simultaneously swept water over Charlotte. "Hey, have some sulphur springs, been gushing out of the earth for thousands of years!"

"The earth provides." She laughed and splashed him back before he was able to move out of reach, his feet slipping.

"Where are my bearings?" he shouted. All around him, the pool's surface moved, shimmering, sparkling, reflecting, blinding, dizzying, disorientating. Within moments, he lost Charlotte amongst crowded bodies, old and young, singles and couples, large and small, fat and thin, light and dark, jumping in and climbing out, families clutching babies, the air filled with laughter, screams, the occasional weeping of a child… it seemed that all humanity was in action.

He tried to swim with a purpose. He had to have direction in spite of watery collisions. After several efforts, he came across Charlotte. "This going's a bit heavy. It's like being drunk. I think I need to stop. Why not meet me later, outside, say in about an hour? We have lots of time before the evening train. Let's join each other on that hilltop, up there by that clump of trees in front of the woodland. I might just lie in the grass and bask in contemplation."

"Sure, see you there," she said. "I'll swim for a while longer, as best I can."

He dried, changed and began to walk slowly further up the hillside. With each step, the views around him widened. Far away, across the valley, the surrounding hills were covered by other pinewoods, their branches swaying idly in the afternoon breeze, an ever-moving, restless greenery. As his route gained altitude, he breathed more deeply, felt freer.

At his chosen location, he laid down on the grass, sheltered by pine tree branches overhead. Around and beyond him, the wind continued to rustle millions of blades of grass which covered the rise, fall, curve and indentation of the land, making all parts of the earth move together under the sky, with himself at the centre.

He relaxed. Just a bit tired… could have been those steps up on the Diana Tower… or maybe the pool water… or both… so hot in the sunshine… peaceful… distant pool voices drifting up the hillside… faint hooting of cars from the valley… can almost hear the earth moving… stretch more… good to stretch… sun on body… relaxing… no arthritis… no aching in neck, shoulders, hips, knees… miracle water… don't be silly… move to check again… bit heavy… press into the ground… eyes close tight… red… red… flicker eyes… kaleidoscope… colours changing… white… white of snow falling outside the sanatorium windows… room full of flowers… nearly ninety years ago… I was so happy, my mother said… I hummed from the Appassionata to you, and you gurgled… I was thinking of my own mother, she said… Hungarian farmer's daughter who learnt to speak six languages… writing articles for the *Prager Tagblatt* before marrying that Austrian officer… Mother was so proud of me, their daughter following studies in Vienna… asking me if Freud was a good lecturer and if Franz Lehar's waltzes were a delight… both my parents so happy seeing me marry your father after he'd finished his medical degree at Prague University… seeing us become such good partners at work as well as at home… our existence already set out for us… honeymooning in Merano, skiing in Cortina, the European travels, the habits of the spa town, hillside pool swimming, tennis, theatre and concert going, forest walking… a life, she said, in which we produced a son for a future which we could never have imagined… colours… colours again… Prague with Mother in that green dress under red, white and black swastikas… London grey… raining grey… Richmond Park hedgerows of purple and brown… collecting autumn firewood with Father along those lines of trees… Buckinghamshire with black and red of that second-hand Morris Eight and the silver of that third-hand bicycle… settling… settling… another country taking us in… only the briefest of hesitations, then warmth of ready acceptances… do meet us, do join us, do be a part of us, part of our communities, our organisations, our places of work, our places of learning, our places of worship… just follow your own directions, you are free now… no more knocks on the door in the middle of the night… overwhelming relief and gratitude… such energy moving forwards, taking me with them… colour, colour again… a wedding group, my bride in white, my grey and blue tweed suit… khaki to follow soon… fresh faces of children merging into faces of grandchildren… still warm… bit tired… clouds scattering across sky… white building blocks… Charlotte's face high cheekbones and blue eyes… when is she coming… soon be here… why do I need her so much, always been so self-reliant, but now… was it all worthwhile… all those efforts, all that striving in those blinks of time, in those specks of dust which return to dust… of what use was I to anyone, what if any effect did I have on anything… can I claim to have inspired or even influenced any of my students who were themselves only specks of dust... can I claim to have shaped my children and grandchildren for the better or was I too engrossed in my work... in the pleasure of drawing and designing... was there too much of that first person singular, of that Napoleonic 'I-myself' tendency *what is the world, O soldiers, it is I*... no conflict for him then... did I try enough... did I love others enough... aren't all our lives measured by the presence or absence of love... don't all the songs and sayings speak the truth, *without love you're nothing, nothing at all*... people know that the love of a mother and of parents sets you up for life no matter what troubles hit you... the love of a partner and of children strengthens you, keeps you alive... nations, too, need to remember even wider love, *we must love one another or die*, Auden reminded us even as he took that ship for America, even as the guns began to sound in our little corner of the world and the shooting began and the people began to move, always moving, my mother among them, with little Jan trailing and skipping behind and jumping over the open suitcases, the strings unwinding from the packages, the scattered clothes, the walking sticks, those walking sticks, the old people who had fallen to the ground, so many of them there in the crowd in the middle, the confusion, the desperation, the panic... *being trodden on... must get up again now... must move on... last chance, try again... must avoid not left behind... hold on, must survive, must reach forward... wanting to... having to... escape*... waves of exodus... ever was ever now ever will be... always like this somewhere in good to bad, loving to hating, constructing to destroying, all levels between... bit colder now... not so sunny… push arms into grass… heavy… children crying on the hillside… Charlotte coming soon… press against earth… my earth… foreign land now… world of forest and snow… my hometown… learnt first nursery rhymes here… *tlůče bubeníček, tlůče na buben / a svolává chlapce, chlapci podjdte ven / zahrejem si na vojáky / máme flinty a bodáky / hula, hura, hej / nikdo nemeškej /…* so cheerful… such dark undertones… so Czech… how I liked my little drum slung on my shoulder when walking with father… cool now… head in soft grass… beautiful grass moving in wind… calm now… grass rustling… boughs swaying… wait gently… must look ahead now, she will soon be here soon be with me… can't stop… still time… train waiting… I know it… all is so good.

Acknowledgements

I AM INDEBTED to Miriam Beza, Rita Benton, Diane Hutton, Ruth Martin, Mary McKean, John McKean, Ursula Robson, David Robson and Brendan Ward, all of whose combined insights and comments have strengthened earlier versions of this narrative. My thanks again to Ruth Martin for helping me to survive the practicalities of the internet. My warm appreciation goes to Lenka Kadičikovà for correcting Czech wording and for helping to add the moving nursery rhyme 'Hra na vojàky', verses of which both she and I remember singing in the different years of our respective schooldays. I am especially grateful to Lauren Stenning for her editorial work on the final draft.

Calendar History

1938

12th Sep – Nuremberg rally.

29th Sep – The Munich Agreement (Chamberlain, Daladier, Hitler, Mussolini).

10th Oct – Germany annexes Sudetenland.

1939

15th Mar – Germany invades Czechoslovakia.

1st Sep – Germany invades western Poland.

3rd Sep – Britain and France declare war on Germany.

17th Sep – Russia invades eastern Poland.

27th Sep – Poland surrenders.

1940

9th Apr – Germany invades Denmark and Norway. 'Weser Day'.

10th May – Germany invades Belgium, Holland, Luxembourg and northern France.

15th May – Holland surrenders.

27th May – Dunkirk evacuation begins. UK 'Armada' of eight hundred vessels.

28th May – Belgium surrenders.

4th Jun – Dunkirk evacuation ends.

10th Jun – North African campaign begins.

25th Jul – 'Battle of Britain' begins.

7th Sep – 'The Blitz' begins. 'Black Saturday'.

27th Sep – Germany, Italy and Japan sign 'Triple Alliance'.

31st Oct – 'Battle of Britain' ends.

5th Nov – Roosevelt re-elected for unprecedented third term.

1941

16th May – 'The Blitz' ends.

22nd Jun – Germany breaks non-aggression pact and invades Russia.

14th Aug – Churchill and Roosevelt publish 'Atlantic Charta': a post-war world vision.

5th Dec – Russian counter-offensive begins.

7th Dec – Japan bombs Pearl Harbor, Hawaii.

8th Dec – America declares war on Japan.

11th Dec – Germany and Italy declare war on America. America declares war on Germany and Italy.

25th Dec – Britain surrenders Hong Kong to Japan.

1942

15th Feb – Britain surrenders Singapore to Japan.

29th Apr – Japanese control Burma.

4th Jun – American victory at Battle of Medway. A war turning point.

Sep/Oct – Germany and Russia battle at Stalingrad.

23rd Oct – Allies launch North African offensive. El Alamein.

19th Nov – Russia launches Stalingrad counter-offensive.

1943

1st Feb – Americans force Japanese evacuation from Guadalcanal.

2nd Feb – German army capitulates at Stalingrad. A war turning point.

13th May – Allied victory in North Africa. Axis armies retreat to Sicily.

9th Jul – Allied invasion of Sicily. Operation Husky. A war turning point.

8th Sep – Italy surrenders.

1944

6th Jun – 'D-Day' invasion. Americans, British and Canadians land in Normandy for liberation of north-east Europe.

22nd Jun – British, Indian and Commonwealth troops defeat Japanese at the Battle of Kohima ('The Stalingrad of the East'). A war turning point.

7th Nov – Roosevelt re-elected for unprecedented fourth term.

1945

4th Feb – Yalta conference (Churchill, Roosevelt and Stalin). A plan for post-war Germany.

13th/14th Feb – British and American bombing of Dresden.

19th Feb – Americans invade Iwo Jima.

22nd/23rd Mar – British and American forces cross the Rhein at Oppenheim.

27th Mar – Western allies pause European advance to allow Russians to take Berlin.

9th Apr – Hitler orders execution of pastor Dietrich Bonhoeffer.

10th Apr – Buchenwald liberated by American army.

12th Apr – Roosevelt dies. Harry S Truman elected as new President.

15th Apr – Bergen-Belson liberated by British Army.

16th Apr – Battle of Berlin begins (seven Russian armies involved).

25th Apr – American and Russian troops first meeting at River Elbe.

28th Apr – Mussolini executed by Italian partisans.

29th Apr – Dachau liberated by American army. Hitler marries Eva Braun.

30th Apr – Hitler and Eva Braun suicides.

1st May – Goebbels family suicides.

1st/2nd May – Berlin surrenders (General Helmuth Weidling to General Vasily Chuikov).

4th May – Germany surrenders to General Montgomery at Lünebürg Heath.

7th May – German signing of unconditional surrender in Reims, France.

8th May – VE Day. Victory in Europe Day. Celebrations.

9th–11th May – Russian Red Army enters/takes Prague.

June – War in Pacific continues.

26th Jun – United Nations Charter signed.

17th July– Potsdam Conference (Churchill, Truman and Stalin). Insistence on unconditional surrender of Japan.

26th Jul – Labour wins UK general election. Clement Attlee, PM.

6th Aug – American B29 bomber 'Enola Gay' drops first atomic bomb, 'Little Boy', on Hiroshima.

9th Aug – American B29 Bomber 'Bockscar' drops second

atomic bomb, 'Fat Man', on Nagasaki. Russia declares war on Japan and invades Manchuria.

15th Aug – Emperor Hirohito broadcasts surrender of Japan. VJ Day. Victory over Japan Day. Celebrations. Overall end of the Second World War.

20th Nov – Nuremberg war trials begin. Twenty-four Germans charged.

31st Dec – British Home Guard disbanded.

1946

29th Apr – Tokyo War Crimes Tribunal begins. Twenty-eight Japanese charged.

19th Jun – Beneš formally elected as Czech president (his second term).

1st Oct – Nuremberg trials end.

Twelve sentenced to death.

Three imprisoned for life.

Four imprisoned short term.

Five acquitted.

1948

3rd April – The Marshall Plan starts American economic aid to Western Europe.

9th May – New Communist Constitution in Czechoslovakia. Beneš refuses to sign.

7th Jun – Beneš resigns as president.

3rd Sept – Beneš dies.

24th Nov – Tokyo Trial ends. Seven sentenced to death. Eighteen imprisoned. Seven died during trial.

1949

Germany is divided:

Eastern zone: the German Democratic Republic.

Western zone: the Federal Republic of Germany.

1951

4th May – Festival of Britain begins. A celebration of arts, sciences and technology.

1953

5th Mar – Stalin dies.

1965

24th Jan – Churchill dies.

1968

5th Jan – The Prague Spring begins, ending forty years of communist control.

2016

29th Jul – The Brexit referendum: United Kingdom votes to leave European Union.

2019

28th June–6th July – Fifty-fourth Karlovy Vary Film Festival.

A Czech Nursery Rhyme

'Hra na vojáky'

Tlůče bubeníček, tlůče na buben,
a svolává chlapce, chlapci pojďte ven!
Zahrajem si na vojáky,
máme flinty a bodáky!
Hola, hura, hej,
nikdo nemeškej!

Vezměte své tašky a své ručnice,
připněte si k boku ostré šavlice!
Zahrajem si na vojáky,
máme flinty a bodáky!
Hola, hura, hej,
nikdo nemeškej!

Do řady se stavme, malí vojáci,
a budeme někdy hodní jonáci!
Zahrajem si na vojáky,
máme flinty a bodáky!
Hola, hura, hej,
nikdo nemeškej!

Zde je břeh u cesty, jako pevný hrad
toho dobudeme beze všech útrat!
Zahrajem si na vojáky,
máme flinty a bodáky!
Hola, hura, hej,
nikdo nemeškej!

'Playing soldiers'

Beating drummers, beat the drum,
and call the boys, boys come out!
Let's play at soldiers,
we have flints and bayonets!
Hola, hura, hey,
nobody delay!

Take your bags and your rifles,
clip sharp sabres to your side!
Let's play at soldiers,
we have flints and bayonets!
Hola, hura, hey,
nobody delay!

Let's get in line, little soldiers,
and we will sometimes be
worthy of the Joneses!
Let's play at soldiers,
we have flints and bayonets!
Hola, hura, hey,
nobody delay!

Here is the shore by the road, like a
solid castle,
we will conquer it without any effort!
Let's play at soldiers,
we have flints and bayonets!
Hola, hura, hey,
nobody delay!

Tam stojí bodláčí: Hej na ně spolu!	That's where the thistles stand: hey,
To my posekáme: Všem hlavy dolů!	at them together!
Zahrajem si na vojáky,	We're going to mow them down:
máme flinty a bodáky!	heads down!
Hola, hura, hej,	Let's play at soldiers,
nikdo nemeškej!	we have flints and bayonets!
	Hola, hura, hey,
	nobody delay!

Utíká zajíček, má před námi strach;	The bunny is running, afraid of us;
běžet ho necháme, ušetříme prach.	let him run, save the dust.
Zahrajem si na vojáky,	Let's play at soldiers,
máme flinty a bodáky!	we have flints and bayonets!
Hola, hura, hej,	Hola, hura, hey,
nikdo nemeškej!	nobody delay!

Sedě teď na bobku stříhá ušima;	He is sitting with his ears on his back
snad se nám vysmívá ta čtveračina?	now;
Zahrajem si na vojáky,	perhaps he is mocking us?
máme flinty a bodáky!	Let's play at soldiers,
Hola, hura, hej,	we have flints and bayonets!
nikdo nemeškej!	Hola, hura, hey,
	nobody delay!

My ho potrestáme, neuteče zdráv,	We will punish him, he will not run
nu zajíce střelme: Pif a puf a paf!	away healthy,
Zahrajem si na vojáky,	shoot the hare: pif and puf and paf!
máme flinty a bodáky!	Let's play at soldiers,
Hola, hura, hej,	we have flints and bayonets!
nikdo nemeškej!	Hola, hura, hey,
	nobody delay!

Zahnali jsme svého již nepřítele:
vítězi se vraťme domu po dole!
Hráli jsme si na vojáky,
složme flinty a bodáky!
Až pak bude čas,
zahrajem si zas!

We have already chased our enemy:
let's get back to the house!
We played soldiers,
let's fold the flints and bayonets!
And when it's time,
let's play again!